APPLES, ALUMNI & ANIMOSITY

A Dogwood Springs Cozy Mystery

SALLY BAYLESS

Paperback ISBN: 978-1-946034-36-6

Kimberlin Belle Publishing LLC

Contact: admin@kimberlinbelle.com

Publisher's Note: This is a work of fiction. Names, characters, places, and incidents are a product of the author's imagination. Locales and public names are sometimes used for atmospheric purposes. Any resemblance to actual people, living or dead, or to businesses, companies, events, institutions, or locales is completely coincidental.

Cover art by DLR Cover Designs, www.dlrcoverdesigns.com.

Chapter One

"LIBBY, I'm so happy to see you," called Kate Hoskins, a major donor to the Dogwood Springs History Museum where I served as director. She waved as I climbed out of my car at the Witley Historic Orchard and Retreat Center.

"I'm happy to see you too." I opened a door to the back seat, and my golden retriever, Bella, bounded out with her tail wagging.

The rolling hills around us were covered by trees laden with apples, the sky was bright blue, and the temperature was in the low seventies. A gentle breeze rustled the leaves, and birds softly called. It was a perfect early October day to visit an orchard.

"Your presentations are going to be such a fun addition to our twenty-five-year reunion." Kate beamed and walked toward me. Her wavy red hair shone in the late afternoon sun as she bent down to say hello to Bella.

I reached back into the car and pulled out an easel and a stack of enlarged photos I'd mounted on solid backing.

Kate took the photos from me. "Do you need help carrying anything else?"

"No, today's artifact is small." I slid the easel under one arm and patted my oversized purse. "It's in here."

I'd brought along a historic item I thought they would all appreciate—a souvenir spoon from the grand opening of their alma mater, Grove University.

"Come on over and meet everyone." She gestured to a group of people standing near a cluster of picnic tables outside a quaint red barn.

Kate and I walked across the gravel parking lot. Bella explored as far as her leash would allow, sniffing first at the driveway toward the road, then toward an old white farmhouse, which I identified from what I'd read online as the retreat center.

"You know, when you first called me a few weeks ago, I wasn't sure about doing these talks," I said. A small gust of wind sent a smattering of leaves tumbling across the ground and swirled my shoulder-length brown hair across my face. I smoothed it back into place.

"I could tell. It took a bit of a sales pitch to convince you." Kate's brown eyes twinkled. "Luckily, I'm good at those."

She was. Normally, I didn't make presentations at private events this small. But Kate, who ran her family's large real estate firm in Kansas City, had quickly brought me on board with her plan. Here I was at the end of the workday on Monday, just as she'd asked.

Back in college, Kate and her friends had formed their own club, the Society of History Scholars, a group she readily admitted some had called nerdy. They'd leaned into that nerdiness and embraced it, a fact that warmed my heart, not just because they'd discussed history, but also because they'd had the courage to be true to themselves.

When Kate had heard about the Grove University reunion this upcoming weekend, she'd decided their club should reunite and add its own events. First, she'd rented the retreat center at the orchard for them to use for the week. Then she'd convinced me to come out tonight and every morning after breakfast for the rest of the workweek to share a story about one of my favorite historic artifacts from the museum.

She'd even checked with the orchard owners and invited Bella. Kate had met my dog downtown one day when she was visiting Dogwood Springs. I was taking Bella for a walk, and when I'd introduced them, Bella had tipped her head to one side and politely offered her paw to shake, totally charming Kate.

Not that I was surprised. My sweet Bella had never met a stranger. I couldn't imagine a better dog in the whole world. She was incredibly smart, beautiful, and a big furry bundle of love. As we walked, I reached out and patted her back. A rush of warmth encircled my heart. Adopting Bella was one of the best decisions I'd ever made.

"Now that I'm here at the orchard," I said as we neared

the group standing near the picnic tables by the barn, "I'm really excited. I think you had a great idea."

What could be better? The atmosphere was idyllic, and I'd be speaking to a group of history enthusiasts. I'd prepared presentations that could later double as programs for the entire Dogwood Springs community. And then there was Kate's irresistible offer—she'd promised to double her latest generous donation to the museum if I agreed to her plan. As the director of a nonprofit, I'd worked hard to rebuild my life over the past year and a half, so how could I possibly say no to that?

We set my things down on one of the picnic tables.

"Let me introduce Hannah and Noah Porter, the owners of the orchard." Kate gestured to a slender woman with short, tousled dark hair and a tall, bearded man with chestnut hair. "The orchard has been in Hannah's family for more than a hundred years."

"It's beautiful," I said to them. "I'd love to learn more about its early operation. And I've heard your apples and cider are delicious."

They both smiled, and Hannah promised to tell me the history of the orchard.

Bella approached Noah and Hannah, giving them each ample opportunity to pet her.

"Hannah was one of our friends back in college," Kate said, "so we had the privilege of spending time here on weekends when we were at Grove University. I loved coming here every fall to go apple picking."

As always, when I spent time with Kate, I noticed how

closely she paid attention when she talked with people, making each person in the conversation feel important.

"So many great memories from those days," a man with sandy blond hair and a Grove University football letter jacket said as the others moved closer.

"These are the rest of our friends." Kate gestured, then introduced them one by one.

She started with Chad Weaver, the man in the letter jacket, and his wife, Francie, who had long blond curly hair and big blue eyes.

"Chad's a businessman in St. Louis."

"Missouri Fan Gear," he said.

I'd heard that name. "I think I know someone who orders St. Louis Cardinals shirts from you."

"We sell a lot of them." A note of pride rang in Chad's voice, and he stood taller as if bolstered by the recognition.

"And you've probably seen Francie on TV," Kate said. "She's a news anchor on Channel 7 in St. Louis."

Francie fluffed her hair and gave me a look like a benevolent royal. My role as a fan seemed to go without question.

A hint of disapproval flashed through Kate's eyes.

I nodded to the news queen even though I didn't watch the St. Louis station.

Kate turned to a plump woman with hazel eyes and mousy brown hair cut like a mushroom cap. "This is Jessica Evans. She also lives in St. Louis, and she teaches elementary school."

"Fourth grade," Jessica said.

"A great age," I replied. "I always love it when older elementary kids visit the museum."

Jessica gave me a hesitant smile. "At first, I thought I wouldn't be able to be here this week, but it's fall break at my school."

Her words sounded forced. If I had to guess, I'd say she was one of those people who felt comfortable around children, but awkward around adults.

"That did work out nicely." I smiled back at her, trying to put her at ease.

"The timing worked out for me as well." A short man with thinning dark hair adjusted his gold wire-framed glasses. "Our school just began scheduling a fall recess into the academic calendar this year, and I couldn't be more pleased. The students need an opportunity to reconnect with family and rejuvenate for the remainder of the semester. And it gave me the perfect chance to see old friends."

"This is Derek Reed," Kate said. "He's the dean at a liberal arts college in Kansas."

I shook his hand and told myself not to be nervous that I'd be presenting history to an academic.

"Last but not least, Tabitha Tucker." Kate touched the arm of a woman with ash blonde hair and warm brown eyes. "She's also a news anchor, but she lives in Omaha."

"It's nice to meet you," Tabitha said. "I'm looking forward to your presentations."

"I hope you enjoy them." I was struck by the similarities between her and Francie. Tabitha was more rounded than

Francie, who was so thin she seemed almost angular, and her hair was not as light, but their hairstyles and makeup were almost identical.

Bella walked up to each person, head high and eyes shining with delight. She loved meeting new people.

Derek asked her name, and I introduced her. All the alumni responded as I hoped, saying she was beautiful, scratching her ears, and telling her what a good dog she was.

I looked at them, mentally reviewing their names. I knew them now, but I was fairly certain they would all blur in my mind later. "Please forgive me if it takes me a day or two to keep everyone straight."

"Of course," Tabitha said, her voice full of understanding.

Really, the only member of the group who stood out was Francie.

Having come straight from work at the museum, I was dressed up in black pants, a blazer, a blouse that set off my green eyes, and my customary pearls. Aside from Francie, all the others wore jeans and sweaters or casual jackets. Even though Kate's outfit looked expensive, it was still casual, and Tabitha's was particularly stylish with darling little brown boots. Francie, on the other hand, wore a dressy cream blouse, a cream wool poncho, and cream pants, which seemed ill-advised for a picnic.

In addition, according to Kate, the group had met in a freshman history class. If this was their twenty-fifth college reunion, they all had to be about forty-six. Francie, though, looked closer to my age, thirty-three. And was it my imagination, or was her forehead immobile?

I guess Botox wouldn't be unusual for a TV personality in a market as large as St. Louis.

"Ready to get things started?" Noah gave the group a broad smile and held up a stack of small baskets. "We've got four varieties of apples ready for harvest." He handed a basket to each alum. "Fuji, Winesap, Arkansas Black, and a few Jonathans."

He pointed out the sections of the orchard where each variety grew and reminded them to look for apples farthest from the trunk, which would be the ripest, to keep the stem on, and to lift the apple in their palm and gently twist it to remove it from the tree.

Then he angled his head toward a spigot in the yard. "Afterward, you can each rinse off an apple to have with our picnic dinner and keep the rest to snack on throughout your time at the retreat center. Fresh fall apples, straight from the tree. What could be better?"

The alums looked out at the orchard, eyes shining as if energized by his excitement.

"We've got ingredients in the retreat center kitchen if any of you want to bake this week," Hannah said. "My grandma's apple pie recipe is in there along with the cutest apple-shaped wooden chopping board made by a local craftsman."

"I adore baking," Tabitha exclaimed. "I'm headed for the Jonathans. That's what my mother always used in her pies."

Chad and Derek grinned, and I overheard a few comments about how they hoped she planned to share.

"When you come back, Hannah and I will have dinner ready," Noah looked at me. "Libby, if it's okay with you, we'll ask you to give your first talk as everyone starts dinner."

"Sounds perfect," I said.

"After dinner, we'll have a bonfire and a hayride, just like we did so many times back in college," Hannah added.

"This is delightful." Kate drew in a deep breath, her eyes shining. "Hannah, thank you so much for arranging it all. And Libby, thank you for coming."

Everyone else murmured their appreciation, including their thanks to Kate for her role, and the alumni wandered into the orchard, some individually, some in pairs.

I glanced around, getting my bearings for when I'd speak.

Hay bales were stacked in the corners of the picnic area, and red-checkered cloths had been fastened down on three of the five tables—two arranged side by side lengthwise and one centered in front of them.

"We're going back to our house to get the food," Hannah told me. She pointed at a newer, one-story blue house with solar panels on the roof that sat closer to the road. "Please, go ahead and set up for your presentation. I thought everyone could sit at the two tables that are pushed together, and you could stand at the one with the tablecloth that's in front of them."

"Great. I'll run through my talk while you're gone."

I sat at a table and dug my notes out of my oversized purse. Bella flopped down on the pea gravel beside the table, happy to have made new friends. I reviewed my notes, readied my easel so I could quickly set it up, and reminded myself that there was no reason to be nervous simply because Derek was a dean at a college. I had a solid presentation with interesting stories from the early years when Grove University had been Grove College and had primarily served to educate teachers. As an academic, he'd probably be even more interested than the rest.

Fifteen minutes later, Bella got to her feet, her nose aquiver.

Noah and Hannah walked toward us, each carrying a dish.

"Is that fried chicken Bella and I smell?" I asked Noah.

"You guessed it." He chuckled and set a platter in the middle of one of the two picnic tables connected longways.

I shortened Bella's leash to help prevent the temptation to steal a drumstick.

Noah and Hannah made several trips and soon had the food set out family-style. I spotted potato salad, golden ears of corn, a green salad with bright red tomatoes, a charcuterie board, pitchers of iced tea, water, and lemonade, and, of course, the fried chicken.

When we'd talked on the phone, Hannah had asked if I wanted to stay for dinner. I'd declined, clearly a mistake on my part.

After checking the table, Noah rang a large bell on a

metal stand next to the barn. I'd seen bells outside historic one-room schoolhouses that looked almost identical.

"An antique?" I asked Hannah.

"I think it's been here since at least 1938," she replied. "My grandparents used it to call their ten kids to lunch and dinner."

The alumni trickled back, chatting happily and carrying full baskets of fruit. Hannah passed out paper towels, and people gathered around the pump to rinse off apples.

"Does anyone know where Francie is?" Hannah asked.

The alums shook their heads.

"We started off together, but I got sidetracked talking with Tabitha about the year the Grove University football team went 11-0," Chad said.

"It was our senior year," Tabitha added. "Chad was the quarterback."

"I'll text her," Kate said.

When she didn't reply after a few moments, Chad pulled his phone from his pocket. "Let me try calling."

But Francie didn't answer, and she didn't wander out of the orchard.

"Could she be on a call for work?" Derek asked. "Something she needed to discuss in private?"

"Maybe." Chad's forehead creased. "But I'd think she'd have heard the bell and at least come close enough to wave to us."

Noah's eyes tensed and he glanced over at Hannah. "I did think I heard the tractor. She couldn't have ...?"

Hannah shook her head. "I know I told you how funny

we all thought it was back in college that Francie, the city girl, loved driving the tractor. And we do still have the same one that Dad repaired a million times before he and Mom retired to Arizona. But I can't see Francie messing with it now, all these years later."

Noah shrugged. "Yeah, I probably heard a truck on the road. Still, we'd better check. I'd hate for her to have thought she was going to give everyone a laugh by driving the tractor over the hill but accidentally rolled it."

Chad's face grew pale, and the rest of the group exchanged nervous glances.

"Let's split up and look for her," Kate said.

The alumni headed out in pairs, calling out Francie's name.

Noah hesitated for a second, looked back at the blue house, and headed toward it to the southwest. "I think the sound I heard came from this direction."

I gave Bella's leash a gentle tug, went around the old farmhouse, and continued north. "C'mon, girl. We need to find Francie."

Bella trotted to my side as we walked through the orchard. "Francie!" I shouted. I peered through the rich green leaves and down the spaces between the rows.

But I saw nothing but Fuji apples gleaming on the trees, and the orchard was eerily silent. Even the birds had stopped twittering.

Let's see ... The alumni had spent about fifteen minutes picking apples. If Francie walked straight away from the picnic area, she could have gone quite a distance, possibly out of earshot. And we had no idea what direction she might have headed once she left Chad. The orchard covered a lot of acres and—

A loud scream pierced the air.

My heart froze.

I spun, not sure which direction the sound had come from.

Bella, though, gave a loud bark and lunged toward the west. I ran behind her over a small hill.

After another few feet, I saw Tabitha hugging Kate.

Kate looked up at me, her eyes huge. "I couldn't ... I couldn't believe it when I found her."

As I came closer, the rest of the group appeared, running up from all directions.

There, near Tabitha and Kate, sat an old blue tractor straddling Francie's body between its front and back tires.

One of the front tires had rolled past her feet and missed them. But the other front tire had rolled straight across her chest, leaving small clods of dried mud clinging to her cream-colored blouse.

To make matters worse, there was a bloody wound on the side of her head. And it didn't look like she'd gotten that injury by falling and landing on a rock. The space between the orchard rows was grassy.

If I had to guess, I'd say someone had hit her in the head, knocked her out, and driven over her with the tractor.

____

Chapter Two

"FRANCIE!" Chad rushed to where Francie lay partially under the tractor. He knelt beside her, clutching her hand and frantically begging her to respond.

Noah tapped at his phone. "I'm calling 911."

The rest of the group seemed frozen in place, eyes wide, as if they weren't sure what to do.

The sun slipped behind a cloud, and I pulled my blazer tighter around me.

Bella whined and tugged on her leash, peering down at Francie.

One of us needed to check her condition so we'd know what to tell the emergency operator, but Chad was too upset. I glanced around, but no one stepped forward.

"Bella, stay." I looked her in the eye, then knelt next to Chad and pressed two fingers against the side of Francie's throat.

My chest tightened when I didn't feel a pulse.

"Hang on, baby." Chad squeezed Francie's hand and looked at me. "Should we move her?"

"No. We might make things worse." I felt for breath coming out of Francie's nose.

I caught a whiff of Francie's lily of the valley perfume but couldn't feel her breathing.

I pressed my lips together and laid a hand on Chad's arm. "Chad, I'm sorry. I think it may be too late."

He jerked back, covered his mouth with one hand, and moaned. Then he bent down, murmuring to Francie and gently brushing her hair back from her face.

I stood and turned toward the others.

Kate stepped closer to Chad, her chin trembling, and rested a hand on his shoulder.

Tabitha's face had gone pale, her body rigid.

I got up, walked over to Bella, praised her for staying when I'd asked, and ran a hand over the soft fur between her ears, hoping to calm both of us. After a few seconds, the tightness in my chest eased slightly.

"Libby, are you ... are you sure she's dead?" the fourth-grade teacher asked. Jessica, that was her name. "That somewhere around here there's a murderer? I mean, I can't see how this can be an accident."

"I'm afraid she is," I said quietly.

Jessica gave a squeaky cry and wrapped her arms around her chest.

Derek patted her shoulder. His face was shuttered, as if somewhere in academia he'd dealt with many crises and learned to stay calm.

"Where's Hannah?" I asked.

"She went to the end of the driveway by the road to make sure the ambulance doesn't miss the turn," Derek said.

Noah, who stood off to one side, moved his phone away from his mouth. "They say they'll be here soon."

The rest of us nodded.

"Who could have done this?" Kate crossed her arms over her stomach and looked at me. "Has there been some sort of maniac on the loose in Dogwood Springs?"

"Things have been quiet around here lately." I didn't mention that there had been trouble in town a couple of months ago. It had been resolved.

"It's not some random killing," Noah said. "You're the only people at the orchard this afternoon."

Chad's head jerked up, and Jessica seemed to shrink into herself. Tabitha looked even paler.

"None of us would have killed Francie," Kate said.

"I'd say one of you had to." Noah stepped back, his focus returning to the 911 operator.

The alumni stared at each other. An uncomfortable silence stretched, broken only by a sniffle from Jessica.

Finally, a siren sounded in the distance. It grew louder and then was joined by a second, fainter wail.

Bella and I walked to the top of a small hill where we could see better.

Soon an ambulance turned into the driveway. Noah ran over to meet it near the barn and pointed to where it could park closest to Francie's body.

The paramedics climbed out and dashed toward her, and a big gold SUV, emblazoned with "Blaine County Sheriff," drove in and parked beside the ambulance.

A man in a tan uniform climbed out. He squared his shoulders, ran a hand over the gun in his side holster, tipped back his cowboy hat, and followed the paramedics.

Good grief. He looked like the Wild West version of a detective I knew from the Dogwood Springs Police Department, John Harper. Same tightly drawn mouth, same bushy eyebrows.

The sheriff, though, was much younger—maybe in his late twenties. His hair was dark brown, not gray, and his muscles were bulkier.

Plus, there was that hat. And more swagger.

I walked toward the others and, when I got close enough, I squinted and silently read the nameplate under his badge. "Sheriff Billy Harper." I guess we were outside the jurisdiction of the town's police force.

The sheriff strode toward Noah. "What happened here?"

"Thanks for coming, Billy." Noah cleared his throat and then, with more composure than most people could have mustered, explained how the apple picking had gone terribly awry. He pointed at Francie and Chad.

"Francie Weaver, from Channel 7?" the sheriff asked.

"Yep. Libby said she's dead." He gestured toward me.

"Libby?" the sheriff turned to me, eyes narrowed.

I raised a hand halfway. "Libby Ballard, sheriff. I was here to give a history presentation for the group."

"Good Lord," he muttered, mostly to Noah but loudly

enough that everyone heard. "Uncle John told me about her. The last thing I need is some nosy busybody who thinks she's an amateur detective."

My cheeks grew hot.

The sheriff walked over to the paramedics.

I might be a bit nosy, at least according to my ex-husband, and I admit I could be stubborn when I was trying to figure something out, but I was not a "busybody."

And, of course, I didn't intentionally eavesdrop on the sheriff's conversation with the paramedics. But I did walk closer, and it was clear from how they shook their heads that I had been correct.

Francie Weaver was dead.

The sheriff spoke into his radio. Then he walked over to Chad, gently told him that the paramedics had been unable to save Francie, and expressed his sympathies.

Chad's face crumpled, and he turned away. I could tell that deep down, he'd been hoping I was wrong.

I had too.

The other alums surrounded Chad, all expressing their sympathy.

"Hold on there," the sheriff said. "Folks, I'm going to need to talk to each one of you. Until I'm done with those interviews, I'll need you to remain silent. Why don't you sit down at those tables near the barn?" He motioned toward them.

Derek patted Jessica on the shoulder again and angled his head toward the barn. They started walking, and Kate and Tabitha followed. After another second staring at the murder scene, I did as well. The sheriff followed us.

"I'll have to ask you to bear with me," the sheriff said after we'd sat down. "The coroner is on the way, and I've got deputies coming to help. They're headed in from the north end of the county, though, so it'll take a while." His eyes narrowed at the food on the table. "I don't think anybody was poisoned. I don't see any reason why you can't have some lemonade or even eat something if you'd like. Sometimes a little food is good after a shock."

He was right. I had to respect him for mentioning it, and for how kind he'd been with Chad. Despite his comment about me, he seemed like he was trying to help.

Soon, six of us were sitting at the two picnic tables with food. Chad eventually joined us. He was subdued, but except for a comment under his breath that he could use a stiff drink, he was holding it together.

A few moments later, Hannah arrived from the end of the long driveway. The sheriff spoke quietly with her, and her eyes filled with tears. Without a word, she went around the table and hugged Chad, then went to sit by her husband.

While the sheriff watched, we passed around the bowls and platters of food, as well as the iced tea, water, and lemonade. No one put much on their plate except for Tabitha, who took an ear of corn, several cubes of cheese from the charcuterie board, and a giant pile of potato salad.

Stress eating. I'd done it myself—though not after seeing a dead body.

I stuck with lemonade and fed Bella a few cubes of cheese. She sniffed near the table when the fried chicken was passed, but I thought it would upset her stomach. I took an extra plastic cup when they came around, filled it with water, and held it out for her to lap up a drink.

Once she was done, she lay down beside me.

"Is the sheriff related to John Harper, the detective in town, and Wes Harper, the Dogwood Springs police chief?" I whispered to Hannah.

"Billy's the son of their brother, Charles, the former sheriff, who passed away not that long ago," she replied.

The sheriff cleared his throat loudly and glared at me.

I stopped talking.

Besides the tables where we sat, there were three remaining tables. One was in front of us only a couple of feet away, where I would have given my presentation. The other two were behind us, and one of them stood in a big puddle. The sheriff chose the one behind us without the puddle, which put him right behind me.

Perfect for me to listen in.

If I were so inclined.

Which would not in any way make me a busybody. Simply curious.

One by one, the sheriff began calling people over to his table starting with Chad, then Tabitha.

And I heard every word.

He didn't ask all the questions I would have, though, like if each of them was alone when Francie died. But I had the feeling he wouldn't welcome suggestions from me.

In the end, I didn't learn anything interesting about either Chad or Tabitha, but after the sheriff finished with Tabitha, two deputies walked over to him. The sheriff told them that everyone on the property except for the paramedics was a suspect, and he instructed them to begin gathering evidence.

Next, he called Noah over to his table. After some routine questions, he asked Noah if he had anything more to add.

"You know, at first I thought that whoever killed Francie had to be one of the alums who are visiting," Noah said. "I realized there's another possibility."

My ears perked up.

"Over the past couple of weeks, we've had a trespasser. They've been stealing apples, leaving the cores tossed on the ground after they eat them, and sneaking around. I've tried to catch the guy, but he's fast."

"You're sure it's a guy?" the sheriff asked.

"Pretty sure. I only got a glimpse of him. But I can tell you that he eats apples almost down to nothing."

"Thanks, Noah. That's a good lead," the sheriff said.

Why would some random trespasser on the orchard property kill Francie? That seemed hard to believe. Unless she saw him doing something illegal—

"Libby?" the sheriff called. There was a note of annoyance in his voice.

Yikes. Had he called my name before, and I been so busy thinking that I hadn't heard him? "Stay, Bella." I pointed to the ground beside me.

I scurried over to sit across from the sheriff. He took down my name and contact information and had me explain again why I was at the orchard.

"How well do you know these people?" he asked.

"I know Kate Hoskins because she's a major donor to the Dogwood Springs History Museum." I'd already told him that I was the director. "She's the one who invited me. The one who arranged all of this, I think."

He scribbled a note on his pad and asked me to describe what had happened.

I did as he requested, giving a good deal more detail than Chad or Noah or Tabitha.

The sheriff wrote down everything I said, even asking me to repeat a thing or two. "Why were you the one who determined the victim was dead? Do you have medical training?"

"Uh, no." Why *had* I felt compelled to check to see if Francie had a pulse? "I wanted to see if there was anything we could do for her."

The sheriff ran his fingertips over the brim of his cowboy hat and narrowed his eyes at me. "And you knew what to do because crime follows you around like a curse, doesn't it?"

"I have been unfortunate in that way since I moved to Dogwood Springs," I mumbled.

He sat back and his chest swelled. "Now listen up, Miss Ballard. I've heard about your sleuthing from my uncle, John Harper. Even heard about your dog, who's supposed to be so smart." He glanced over at Bella with what might have been a flicker of respect. "My uncle's been a lot more tolerant of your interference than I would ever be. I'm telling you in no uncertain terms that you need to keep your nose completely out of my investigation. Do you understand?"

I nodded.

"Solving crimes in the county is my job, not yours. You need to stick to telling those history stories and raising money for the museum, or I'll arrest you for interfering with an ongoing investigation and toss you in the county jail." He made a shooing motion with his hand.

I sat back down beside Bella.

"Sheriff?" Chad raised a hand. "I heard what Noah said about the trespasser."

The sheriff stiffened as if perhaps he hadn't thought about all of us sitting there, listening.

"It got me to thinking," Chad continued. "Francie does get some crazy fans. Like this one guy who claimed he was in love with her. Thought that when he saw her on TV, she was really in his living room." His jaw tightened. "I told her not to post anything about this trip on social media, but she wanted to give Hannah some publicity, so she mentioned that she planned to come here in October. Probably not that long before the trespasser showed up here."

The sheriff scribbled on his pad. "An excellent tip. Did the authorities identify that guy, the one who thought he was in love with her?"

"Oh, yeah," Chad said. "It wouldn't be him. I was thinking maybe some other crazy."

The sheriff looked back up. "Had she mentioned any social media messages or texts or calls that seemed suspicious recently?"

Chad shook his head.

The sheriff frowned and stood. "Ma'am?" He gestured to Kate. "Let's talk over there, on the porch of the retreat center."

Kate followed the sheriff over to the porch.

No more listening in.

Eventually, Kate returned, and the sheriff interviewed Jessica and then Derek, both on the porch.

At last, the sheriff walked back over and told Noah and Hannah that the orchard would need to be closed until they had finished collecting evidence. Hannah's face grew rigid, but they both agreed.

Next, the sheriff told all the alumni that they would need to remain in town until he wrapped up his investigation.

"But what if we don't want to stay out here at the orchard where there's a murderer on the loose?" Tabitha asked.

"It's fine with me if you move to a hotel in town," the sheriff said. "You just need to let my office know where you'll be."

Noah and Hannah exchanged glances.

"Uh, Tabitha," Hannah said. "You can check around if you like, but I've had a lot of calls lately. I think every room in town is booked for the reunion. I mean, you might be able to move away for a day or two, but later in the week, you'd have to move back."

"She's probably right." Derek made a pained expression. "Grove University sent out an email last week, and I noticed their alumni events coordinator was listing hotel space in towns forty-five miles away."

"Nobody's going forty-five miles away," the sheriff said.

Hannah and Noah whispered to each other and motioned the sheriff aside with them.

A minute later, he turned back to the group. "The orchard has a honeymooner's cottage that's being renovated and hasn't been rented out yet. I'll have a couple of my deputies stay there. They can take turns doing patrols, day and night."

There was some grumbling from the alumni, but the sheriff didn't offer them much choice.

Thankfully, Bella and I lived in town and were allowed to go home. And, as I stood, Kate whispered to me that I shouldn't even think about a presentation the next day.

For the time being, the Witley Historic Orchard and Retreat Center would be home to two sheriff's deputies, owners Hannah and Noah, and guests Chad, Tabitha, Derek, Jessica, and Kate.

As Chad said, the killer could be someone we didn't know, someone who'd been waiting around the orchard for days for the chance to kill Francie. But, since Francie hadn't mentioned any unusual contact from her fans lately, it seemed like a long shot.

Most likely, one of the alums was a murderer.

Chapter Three

AS SOON AS I pulled into my driveway, I spotted my best friend, Cleo Anderson, near our detached garage. Cleo rented the top floor of our white two-story home, and I had the first-floor apartment.

The house was nothing fancy—a place most people would describe as old rather than historic, and updates over the years had been serviceable, not upscale. But it had more character than a cookie-cutter apartment, the lot had big trees, and in renting there, I'd met both Cleo and Bella, two of the best parts of my life in Dogwood Springs.

"Hey, Libby," Cleo called as I got out to open my side of the double garage.

I gave her a weak wave.

"Are you okay?" The long bangs of Cleo's blond pixie cut fell forward as she set a paintbrush down on a piece of plastic sheeting. Then she stood, scooted her oversized glasses up her nose with the back of her hand, and walked closer.

"Not really. Let me park and I'll fill you in."

Cleo was two years younger than me, and we were one of those pairs of friends whose bond was stronger because of our differences. I was quieter and more serious, a planner and logical thinker who dressed rather traditionally. Cleo was creative, dramatic, a swirl of bright colors, and sometimes a little loud. She was tall and trim, a bundle of energy whose brown eyes usually sparkled. When I'd moved in, she'd eagerly welcomed me and quickly became one of the best friends I'd ever had. After the shock of the murder, I felt a little better just seeing her.

Once I let Bella out of the car and shut the garage door, I joined Cleo at the side of the garage where she had lined up paint rollers and brushes.

"I was setting things out to dry." Cleo bent down to pet Bella. "I spent the whole day painting at the apartment over my salon. It's not the most relaxing way to spend my day off, but that place needs a lot of work."

I nodded. She'd recently bought the building that housed her hair salon downtown. "You know Francie Weaver, the news anchor on Channel 7 from St. Louis?"

"Yeah. Channel 7's not my favorite, but I watch it sometimes." Cleo leaned down and patted Bella.

"I was giving the first of those history talks at the orchard. Before we started, the orchard owners let the alumni go into the orchard to pick some apples for snacks.

Francie didn't come back. Someone hit her in the head and then ran her over with the tractor."

Cleo's mouth fell open.

"Come on into my apartment." I motioned toward the house. "I need to feed Bella."

Cleo followed me, and I filled in more details as I gave Bella her dinner, which she gobbled down as if her dinnertime had been delayed days rather than a couple of hours.

I let out a long sigh and for the first time since we'd found Francie's body, I finally began to feel calm.

"Poor Hannah." Cleo leaned back against the edge of the kitchen counter. "I don't know her husband very well, but this has to be horrible for her, having a friend murdered at the orchard."

"Do you also know the sheriff, Billy Harper?"

Cleo rolled her eyes. "I know him."

"He made it very clear that he doesn't want me getting involved. Which is fine with me."

Sort of.

I did feel like I should try to help. After all, I'd been there when the poor woman was killed.

Cleo raised an eyebrow. "You're not going to investigate? You've only lived in Dogwood Springs a year and a half, so maybe you don't follow county politics that closely. Billy only got elected because his dad was the sheriff."

I bit my lip, then shook my head. "I didn't know that, but my answer's still no." Just because I'd had success solving local murders in the past didn't mean I should get involved now. "I didn't know Francie. The murder didn't take place at the museum or at a museum event. Yeah, I was at the orchard to give a history talk, but that's not the same thing."

"Are you sure?"

"I'm more than happy to let Billy Harper investigate this all on his own."

Cleo narrowed her eyes and tipped her head to one side. "You staying out of a murder investigation in Dogwood Springs? I'll believe it when I see it."

The next morning offered another picture-perfect fall day. After I took Bella for a walk and got her settled for the morning, I headed down the sidewalk to work.

The air was crisp and refreshing, and after ten minutes, I reached the edge of downtown Dogwood Springs, which was awash in everything autumn. Chrysanthemums clustered near every shop door. The red maples that lined both sides of the street were ablaze with color. The scent of pumpkin spice filled the air, and a chalk sandwich board outside the bakery announced that apple muffins had been delayed but would be available after nine.

It really was a lovely town. Because of the tourist trade, it boasted several upscale restaurants, and Main Street was lined with charming shops. My favorite was an accessory shop called "It Always Fits," but I was also quite fond of other downtown offerings—the three-story library, the independent bookstore, and, of course, the museum. Away from downtown, on the southern end of Dogwood Springs, Grove University was its own little world. Outside the city limits, gentle hills surrounded the town, and back roads led to a local winery, the beautiful springs the town was named for, and the orchard.

As I strolled along, I did my best to push past thoughts of the murder. I promised myself a muffin after I walked home to let Bella out at lunchtime, and I stopped to send my landlord a text about a drip in my kitchen faucet. Then I walked toward the Dogwood Springs History Museum at the far end of Main Street.

The museum, originally built in 1920 as the home of local businessman Charles Pennington, was a white two-story Greek revival that looked disproportionately large for its lot. Pennington, from what I'd read, had wanted to impress not just the neighbors but any visitors from St. Louis or Kansas City.

Fortunately for the town, he'd also wanted to be remembered. He'd left his home to be used as the Dogwood Springs History Museum and set up a trust fund that provided for my salary and that of two additional paid staff.

Fortunately for me, I had the best staff members a museum director could hope for: Curator Rodney Grant and Education Coordinator Imani Jones.

As I entered the back door of the museum, a wave of peace washed over me. Maybe it was what I thought of as the smell of history—lemon furniture polish, slightly musty paper, and a hint of mothballs. Or maybe it was the knowledge that the entire purpose of the building was to provide access and inclusion so that all could learn about the past. Hopefully, in understanding it more fully, they'd understand themselves and the modern world a little better. Whatever the cause, my chest felt more expansive each time I stepped into the building.

Down the hall, I heard voices. I walked through the conference room, which had been the original kitchen of the museum, and into the gift shop, where Rodney and Imani were unpacking a shipment of T-shirts. Each shirt featured the museum logo on the front but had different messages on the back.

"I'm getting this one," Rodney said. He held up a pale blue shirt that read "So many museums, so little time."

"It's perfect." I beamed at him. All three of us liked to visit other museums, but Rodney, a quiet man in his sixties with a ruddy complexion, kind eyes, and a dry sense of humor, had recently begun logging the museums he visited like a birder keeping track of species. I had expected when I ordered the shirts that he might like that one.

"These are fabulous, Libby!" Imani pushed back her box braids, then held up a bright purple shirt and turned it to show the back, which listed famous Black female inventors throughout history. "I'm getting one for myself and one for each of my nieces for Christmas."

A T-shirt wasn't Imani's typical work attire, which normally ran to 1960s vintage dresses, but I could picture her looking adorable in it. Tall, willowy, and in her late twenties, with her long eyelashes and boundless energy, Imani looked good in anything.

Her brow furrowed. "Why are you here? Shouldn't you be out at the orchard?"

"I'm glad you two like the shirts," I said, "but I've got some bad news." I told them about the murder and then excused myself to go up to my office to call a possible donor.

"So, no more presentations at the orchard this week?" Rodney asked before I left.

I stepped into the hall. "Kate and I only talked about canceling today, but I assume not."

Which was unfortunate. After I'd finally agreed, I'd been quite excited about the artifacts I'd chosen to present.

I stepped back into the conference room to make myself a cup of strong Yorkshire black tea, then climbed the stairs to my office on the second floor. Even in the rooms that were off-limits to the public, a sense of history filled the museum. Sunlight filtered through dark wooden blinds, glinting off the wide, ornate crown moldings and baseboards and my large mahogany desk.

Normally, I loved working in this space. But half an hour later, I hung up the phone, even more dejected. The conversation with the potential donor from Springfield had started out fine when he asked if the museum would be willing to display a few items from a collection of beer cans and beer bottles belonging to a man who'd lived in Dogwood Springs thirty years ago.

I'd told him certainly, if they had a connection to local history.

They didn't. And the more we talked, the worse things got. What the donor really wanted was for the museum to take a collection of more than six thousand beer cans and beer bottles, many of which sounded like they were less than twenty years old. None had a connection to the town —other than possibly having been drunk there—and he wanted a promise that we'd keep every one of them and display them all on a rotating basis.

Um, no.

As delicately as I could, I'd explained that we had a specific mission and a severe lack of storage space. And we required that the items be valued by an independent appraiser. We couldn't simply take his word that the collection was worth $50,000 and give him a tax receipt.

That last part had been the kicker.

The potential donor's response had been loud, angry, and profane.

I spun my chair away from my desk to face the window and stretched out my shoulders. Most people in the world were good, but there were definitely a few bad apples like the would-be beer can donor and the murderer at the orchard.

I was still staring out the window when footsteps neared my office, and someone cleared their throat.

I turned back around.

Hannah stood in my doorway. "Libby? Have you got a moment?"

"Sure." I gestured her in and waved at the chair across from my desk. "How are you doing?"

I regretted the words almost as soon as I said them because I really didn't need to ask. Her hairdo was lopsided, and her eyes had huge dark circles under them.

Hannah shifted in her chair. "Noah and I are hanging in there. It's horrifying having someone killed on our property. And it's even worse since it's someone I knew."

"I can only imagine."

"I went over to my Aunt Alice and Uncle Doug's this morning after breakfast. You know who I mean? Alice and Doug VanMeter."

I blinked. "I didn't realize you were related."

Hannah gave a halfway smile. "Doug is my mom's older brother."

Interesting. Every time I thought I had the interconnections in this town figured out, I realized there were more, even among my closest friends.

"Doug and Alice thought that maybe you might be able to help me."

My stomach tightened ever so slightly. I had a feeling I knew where this was headed.

"I didn't tell Noah I was coming. He doesn't understand —not really—how bad this situation is for the orchard. Money is tight. Maybe a little tighter than I've led him to believe." She scraped a hand through her hair. "The sheriff let us reopen the orchard and the farm market to the public, but if we don't have a steady stream of customers all fall, our biggest season of the year, I'm afraid we might have such a cash-flow problem that we'll have to sell to this guy who wants to cut down all the apple trees and put in a subdivision."

Ouch. That would be criminal in itself. "Surely the sheriff will solve this quickly."

She arched a brow. "Do you really think Billy's capable?"

I opened my mouth to assure her but then thought about what Cleo had said and about the conversations I'd overheard between the sheriff and the alumni. I kept silent.

"You don't have any more confidence in him than I do." Hannah shook her head. "Billy's a nice guy, but he's in over his head. He's new to the job and, yeah, he had some success with minor cases like vandalism, but he's never handled a murder."

Which meant he was trying to prove himself. That might account for the swagger. But swagger wouldn't identify a killer.

I picked up a pen and tapped one end against my desktop, flipped it, tapped the other end, then flipped it again.

Tap. Flip. Tap. Flip.

Did I want to get involved in investigating another murder? I had a museum to run and my own safety to think about.

"Please." Hannah looked across the desk at me, her big hazel eyes filled with a mix of worry and fear. "The orchard's been in business for generations. I don't want to be the one who lets it fail."

I wouldn't either if I were Hannah. And I did feel like I should do something to help.

But ...

My phone rang. I glanced over at where it sat on the desk. My friend Alice's face filled the screen.

"Please, go ahead," Hannah gestured to the phone.

I answered the call, but I didn't put it on speaker.

"Libby, you may not have known, but Hannah is Doug's sister's girl and—"

"She told me. She's right here."

"Oh, I'm sorry," Alice said. "I thought I could talk to you before she arrived. I certainly don't want to put any pressure on you. But I sort of mentioned your name in passing, and she practically ran out the door. I think she's desperate to have this situation resolved."

I heard Doug's muffled voice in the background.

"Doug and I don't want you to feel obligated to investigate," Alice said.

But they wouldn't have mentioned my name if they hadn't been hoping I would help, would they?

Although she was close to my mother's age, Alice was one of my best friends and one of the kindest people I'd ever known. Plus, she was the head of the museum's board of directors, the woman who'd hired me, and the museum's No. 1 volunteer. She was one of those unassuming, capable women who operated behind the scenes, keeping many town organizations running smoothly. And she was so friendly that everyone in town loved her.

And her husband was just as nice. This was their niece, and she needed my help.

And I ... well, I believed in justice. It was part of the fabric of who I'd always been, a value that had been further cemented when I'd been treated unfairly by my ex-husband.

I couldn't stand idly by and let Francie's killer go free because the sheriff didn't know what he was doing.

I set the pen down firmly on the desk and hit the speaker on my phone. "I can't promise anything ..."

Across from me, Hannah sat up taller and her eyes lit. "But you'll try?"

"I'll try."

Hannah's breath came out in a rush. "Oh, thank you."

"Thank you, Libby!" Alice's voice rang out loud and clear over the phone line.

"I'll get back with you soon, Alice," I said into the phone. I hung up.

Hannah stood, and by the time I'd gotten to my feet, she'd rounded the desk and pulled me into a hug. "I can't tell you how much I appreciate this."

"Your aunt and uncle and some other friends have helped me in the past when I looked into other murders. Let me see when they're all available. We'll need you to tell us what you know about everyone who was at the orchard yesterday."

"Just name the time." Hannah picked up a sticky note and pen from the desk and wrote down her cell number.

The phone on my desk rang. I glanced down and recognized the number of a woman who was interested in becoming a volunteer.

Hannah said she should let me get back to work, waved, and hurried out of my office.

It was time to switch back into museum-director mode. But as soon as the call was over, I'd be texting my friends to see if we could meet this evening.

We had a murder to try to solve.

Chapter Four

"WE WON'T all fit at our regular table if Hannah is joining us for dinner. Let's push those two together." Cleo pointed across the outdoor patio at the Dogwood Café.

"Good idea." We were lucky we could all meet tonight. And lucky there were two open tables close together. With the maples just one week away from peak color and the reunion at Grove University coming up, the town was packed with visitors. So far, at least, it seemed they hadn't heard about the murder.

Bella made several stops to say hello to acquaintances old and new as we wound our way across the patio where groups of friends talked and laughed. Cleo and I arranged the green metal tables and chairs, and I showed Bella a spot where she could lie down out of the flow of traffic and away from the portable heaters the café brought out every fall. Later in the evening, those heaters would feel great, but for now, when the sun still hovered near the horizon, the temperature was comfortable with a light sweater. Or, in Bella's case, soft golden fur. She sniffed at a spill on the concrete, then circled twice and lay down.

Cleo and I had just gotten seated side by side facing the entrance when Hannah arrived with Alice and Doug.

Today, as always, Alice looked polished. She wore a burgundy sweater and matching knit pants, and, thanks to Cleo, her chin-length brown hair was styled in a flattering cut that made her look younger than her age in her late fifties. In addition to playing a vital role in many volunteer organizations in town, Alice had recently started taking classes at Grove University, hoping to earn her degree. I sometimes wondered if she was the most formally dressed student in her classes.

Her husband, Doug, who wore tan pants and a cream sweater, had a fringe of gray hair, a short white beard, and an easy smile. He hadn't been involved in all the cases we'd solved because he was frequently out of town dealing with the large online gift-basket business he owned. I knew, though, that I could count on him for keen insight, and I had the feeling that he was a wonderful boss.

I stood and beckoned them over.

"Oh, Libby, thank you for helping Hannah," Alice said.

"We didn't want to impose," Doug added, "but we're so glad you're looking into this."

"I'm happy to help." I gestured to the chairs at the table, and they sat down across from Cleo and me. "After all, figuring out who killed Francie won't simply help the orchard. I don't know about you, but I'd feel a lot safer knowing that the murderer was behind bars."

"Me too," Alice said.

Sam and Zeke joined us, and I introduced them to Hannah.

She seemed a little star-struck meeting Sam, the man I was dating, but I guess I shouldn't have been surprised. After all, he'd owned a computer company in California before he took a position teaching at Grove University, and he was easily the wealthiest man in the county.

He quickly set her at ease. Most of the time, he was so humble and down-to-earth that I didn't even remember how much money he had, just his tenderness, his sense of humor, his curiosity about mysteries, and his patience with me as I slowly grew to trust him. And, of course, the fact that he perfectly fit the description of tall, dark, and handsome. Today, still dressed for the university, he wore tan pants and a French-blue dress shirt that looked great with his dark, wavy hair, chocolate brown eyes, and rectangular black glasses.

Zeke Anderson, the final member of our group, was Cleo's seventeen-year-old nephew and had helped out with every mystery we'd solved. Tall and lean with long dark hair, he wore his trademark black Converse tennis shoes, a faded pair of jeans, and a black sweatshirt with a logo on it that I didn't recognize. If I had to guess, I'd say it had to do with computer gaming. A junior at Dogwood Springs High School, Zeke was smart, logical, and great with computers.

Bella worked her way around the table, greeting each

person, basking in their attention, and nuzzling everyone's legs. Never let it be said that she allowed one of my friends to feel unloved.

After a few moments, I called her over beside me. She'd already eaten, but I gave her one of her favorite doggy treats. Her tags jingled against the concrete as she lay down and began crunching.

As a group, we looked almost like an extended family out for dinner, but we were here to work. As soon as we had ordered, Doug turned to Hannah. "Tell them what you told Alice and me on the way over here."

She glanced at the tourists at nearby tables, but after a second, her shoulders relaxed as if she had decided the patio was too loud for them to overhear her. "The key was in the tractor. But one of the deputies told me that there were no fingerprints on the tractor besides Noah's and mine, only smudges. They think the killer stole Noah's gloves from right inside the door of the barn and wore them when they drove the tractor over Francie."

"Very sneaky," Cleo said.

Our server returned with our drinks, and we sat silent while he distributed them. I unwrapped my tea bag and started it steeping.

Once the server left, Doug gave Hannah a pointed glance. "Tell them the rest."

Hannah shifted in her chair. "I know someone's been sneaking around our property." She pressed her lips together. "But I think I have to accept that the killer is one of my friends. If it was some crazed fan like Chad suggested, I think they'd want to talk to Francie, not murder her."

Cleo and I exchanged glances. Zeke scooted his chair closer to the table, and Sam gave a solemn nod. Hannah's thinking made sense.

"It has to be an awful thing to suspect a friend," I said. "We'll keep the trespasser on our list of suspects just in case, but why don't you tell us about each of your friends?"

Hannah crossed her arms over her chest. "I haven't kept in touch with them a lot, but I can tell you who they were twenty-five years ago."

"That would help," Cleo said.

"OK." Hannah shifted her arms, uncrossing and recrossing them. "Francie, as you all probably know, went into broadcast journalism. If I had to tell you about her back in college, I'd say the best two adjectives are beautiful and bold. She was fearless. It didn't surprise me one bit that she became a big success."

"Bold," Sam agreed. "That's the same word my best friend from elementary school, Victor Dyer, used to describe her."

Doug leaned in. "You know Victor Dyer?"

"Yep." Sam glanced over at me and must have sensed my confusion. "Victor's the weekend sports guy at Channel 7. He worked his way up from smaller stations, and now he's living his childhood dream, covering the best team in Major League Baseball—the St. Louis Cardinals."

Sam and Doug, both avid fans, exchanged grins.

"I texted him when I heard about Francie," Sam continued. "He said about the same thing as Hannah. And said Francie wasn't just a talking head. She was a top-notch investigative journalist, someone who would do anything to get a story."

"Thanks, Sam," I said. "That's good to know."

Alice pulled out a small notepad, wrote the word "Suspects" at the top, added "Trespasser" and made notes about Francie.

"Tell us about the rest of your college friends, Hannah," Doug said.

"Chad Weaver, who Francie married right out of college, is a businessman in St. Louis these days. Back when we were at Grove University, he was incredibly handsome, the football quarterback, and pretty much the big man on campus. He and Francie fit together perfectly."

Alice took a quick sip of her decaf coffee and added Chad to her list.

"Libby," Hannah said, "you know Kate through the museum. She's from a family in Kansas City that's been in real estate for decades, and since she joined the firm, I think it's gotten even bigger. She's great at sales, really connects with people. I can't see her as a killer. Back in school, she was the emotional glue that held our group together, the person each of us wanted to be friends with."

I nodded. I'd known people like that. "What about Jessica?"

"Well, as she told you at the orchard, she teaches fourth grade in St. Louis. In school, she was really shy, and she was kind of on the fringe of our group. I never thought she was that interested in history, but she needed a group of friends, and Kate included her. That was just like Kate."

"What about the guy who's the college dean?" I asked.

"Derek Reed. He majored in psychology and was by far the smartest of the group. I'm not sure I would have passed English lit if he hadn't helped me." Hannah grinned. "I guess it makes sense that he got his Ph.D. He never married, and he's really dedicated to his job. I don't know much about academia, but I think he's kind of a big deal. Oh, and back in college, he had a crush on Francie."

Hannah paused and looked off to one side.

I leaned in. "Is there something else? Even something small might help us."

Hannah shrugged. "She never said anything, but I always thought that Jessica wanted to date Derek."

"Did you notice anything between them at the orchard, dear?" Alice asked.

"No signs of anything romantic. Jessica's been married for years, but they did seem to have fallen back into their old pattern of friendship."

"I'll write that down," Alice said. "Is that everyone?"

"No," Hannah replied. "I haven't mentioned Tabitha. She also went into broadcast journalism. She and Francie were best friends. She works at a TV station in Omaha these days."

Our server arrived with our food, delivering a Cobb salad to Alice, bacon cheeseburgers to Doug, Sam, and Cleo, a fried chicken sandwich to Zeke, and pork tenderloin sandwiches to Hannah and me, hers with dill pickles, mustard and a side of fries, mine with lettuce, mayo, and a side of coleslaw.

Zeke inhaled an enormous bite of his sandwich, looked at Hannah, and then at me. "All these people had an opportunity to kill Francie?"

"Yes," I said. "All the alums went out into the orchard to pick apples. Any one of them could have doubled back to the barn for the gloves, then snuck up on Francie and killed her. I was focused on preparing for my talk. I doubt I would have noticed them."

"Even if you'd been looking, Libby, the barn has a back door," Hannah said.

"Oh." That made me feel better about not spotting the killer. "And all of them knew how to drive the tractor, right Hannah?"

"I taught everyone back when we were in college. It's not that hard."

"This is going to be a challenging case," Sam said. "We don't know any of these people."

"But, other than the trespasser, who we really can't look into, we've only got five suspects." Alice looked at her list. "Chad, the husband. Tabitha, the other broadcast journalist. Derek, the college dean. Kate, the real estate mogul. And Jessica, the elementary school teacher."

Doug leaned forward. "Do you suspect any one of them in particular, Hannah?"

She narrowed her eyes and ran a hand through her hair. "Well, it may seem crazy, but I keep thinking of that crush

Derek had on Francie in college and the fact that he never married. What if he never got over her?"

"But if he was still in love with her, why would he kill her?" Cleo spread her hands palms up and shook her head.

Hannah leaned in. "What if he became obsessed with her and she rejected him? And then he was so angry that he killed her?"

I thought about Derek. I'd only seen him briefly with Francie, but I hadn't picked up on any attraction. And he seemed like a person who was always in control of his emotions.

"Did you see anything odd when they were together?" Alice asked.

Hannah frowned. "Well, no. They both acted normal. No tension or anything, so maybe it's not that good of a theory. But—" She sat up taller. "Hold on. The word *tension* made me think. I overheard a conversation between Chad and Francie. Well, I didn't actually overhear it, not well enough to understand what was said, but enough to hear the tone. I'm not sure they were getting along that well. He seemed so upset when Francie died that I guess I subconsciously decided he was innocent, but maybe that grief was an act."

"The spouse is always a likely suspect." Alice nudged Doug, then winked at him.

I set down my sandwich. "If you picked up on tension between Chad and Francie, maybe they fought, and he was so upset that he killed her."

"It does make sense," Hannah said.

"Then Chad is the person I should talk with first." I wiped some mayonnaise off my fingers. "I just need to figure out how to make that happen."

Our conversation turned to other things, and we finished our meal. As we got ready to leave, Hannah stopped me and thanked me again for helping her.

"No promises," I said, "but I'm trying."

"That means a lot." She hugged me, and we walked out of the fenced-in outdoor seating area together.

On the sidewalk, Sam and Cleo were deep in conversation, and Cleo whispered something about the museum.

Sam nodded.

"Libby's going to love the surprise," Cleo added.

As soon as they noticed me, they stopped talking, but quiet had never been Cleo's forte. Even when she whispered, she was easy to hear.

I was about to ask what was going on when I remembered that a week ago, Sam had seemed interested in a new fundraising campaign I was planning for the museum. Maybe he was planning to make a contribution as a surprise for me.

I smiled and acted as if I hadn't heard anything.

But before I headed home, I couldn't stop myself from hurrying over and giving him a big kiss.

Cleo, Bella, and I walked back to Elm Street, and Cleo described all the Halloween decorations she wanted to put up at our house. Once we got home, I told Bella to go get her ball from the living room. She bolted through the kitchen and quickly returned with the new glow-in-the-dark ball I'd bought her. She dropped it at my feet, let out a happy bark, and nudged me toward the back door. It was fully dark outside, but with the light on over my back step, we played a short game of fetch.

While we played, my mind was halfway on how fun it was to watch Bella jump up and catch the ball in her mouth, and halfway on Francie's murder.

Eventually, the air got cool enough that I called Bella inside. I refilled her water bowl, stretched out on my living room couch, and snuggled under a fuzzy blue throw. After a few minutes, I grabbed my phone off the antique table nearby and sent Kate a text. Would she be interested in me continuing to do the presentations we'd discussed?

My phone rang almost immediately.

"Libby?" Kate sounded excited. "I'd love it if you'd be willing to come out and do the presentations at breakfast. We're going stir-crazy out here."

"That's understandable," I said.

"If you come out and talk about history, it will give us all something else to think about for a while. But are you sure you don't mind? I don't want you to feel like you're in danger."

"Everyone would be together, and one of the deputies would be around. I think it would be fine." I wouldn't feel comfortable wandering in the orchard alone or going to sleep at night in the retreat center, but I didn't mention that. No need to make Kate feel even more uncomfortable.

"That would be wonderful! And oh, is there any chance you'd bring Bella? She's such a sweetie that she's bound to cheer people up."

"I'd love to bring Bella."

We set a time for the next morning and hung up.

Perfect. I'd have a good reason for being at the orchard, and I'd have a deputy there to keep me safe.

Was a deputy enough?

Hmmm. I dug through my purse, looking for my pepper spray.

Found it. And I'd have Bella with me. But I'd feel better if the two of us weren't driving out there alone. Maybe I should also bring a friend.

I ran upstairs and talked to Cleo.

Five minutes later, I was back downstairs, problem solved. I could always count on Cleo. And, as she reminded me, she'd taken self-defense classes back when she lived in New York City. If we could be back in town by a quarter of ten when she needed to open her salon, she'd be happy to go with me.

Tomorrow the two of us would talk to Chad.

Chapter Five

THE NEXT MORNING WAS COOLER, and both Bella and I moved briskly as we took our regular after-breakfast walk down Elm Street to Thirteenth Street and back. Even though Francie had been murdered, it was hard not to smile on what looked like it would be a beautiful fall day, especially with all the cute Halloween decorations my neighbors had on display.

And it was hard not to be happy when Bella was so gentle when a little boy out with his dad wanted to pet her. Or when I played some of my favorite '70s music as Cleo and I drove to the orchard, and we sang along.

The reality of the situation hit home though when Cleo, Bella, and I found Kate waiting on the wooden porch that ran the width of the old farmhouse. She looked like she'd barely slept.

"Thanks again for coming out, Libby," she said as she ushered us inside.

I glanced around, impressed with how they'd kept the feel of the old building with only minor changes. The ceramic tile in the entryway and hall seemed new, as did the soft blue country-style upholstered pieces, but the wooden furniture and the hardwood floors in the adjoining living room and dining room looked original. There was a hint of vanilla in the air and a cozy feel to the decor. The overall impression was that of a restful, comforting place to stay in the middle of a beautiful orchard.

Restful and comforting, that is, unless there had just been a murder.

"I can't wait to see the historical artifact you've brought today." Kate gestured to the alumni, who were all seated around the dining room table, leaving the two ends empty. "Everyone's glad you're here."

I hadn't been sure Chad or Noah would attend, but they both were there, flanking Tabitha on one long side of the table. On the other side, Hannah sat across from Noah, Derek was in the middle, and Jessica sat across from Chad.

Chad looked haggard, but his face softened, and a faint smile broke through when he spotted Bella.

I walked her around the table and reintroduced them.

Bella, who always seemed to have a special intuition for who most needed comfort in a room, sat down right by Chad and rested her head on his thigh.

He stroked her head, and his shoulders relaxed.

Kate sat at the far end, between Chad and Jessica, and motioned for me to take the other end, between Noah and Hannah. A beefy blond guy Kate introduced as Deputy

Miller poked his head in and then leaned against the door-frame to the kitchen behind me. He looked young, even younger than the sheriff, but seemed very alert.

I introduced Cleo as my friend, here to help with the enlarged photos I'd brought. She set up my easel and took a chair in the corner of the room.

In addition to the photos, each of my presentations featured a physical object. After all, people loved learning stories behind artifacts, as my favorite TV show, *Antiques Road Show*, proved.

"Today I want to talk about the role higher education played in the history of the area."

I dug into my oversized purse, pulled out a tissue-wrapped package, and unrolled it.

"This," I said, "is a sterling silver and enamel souvenir spoon from the 1927 grand opening of Grove College, which later became Grove University."

The silver bowl of the spoon showed the first building on campus, which was still called Silersville Hall after the original name of Dogwood Springs. The enamel decoration on the handle displayed the school's crest in sky blue and forest green on a white background.

I passed the spoon around and told them not only about the elaborate reception the college had hosted the fall it opened but also about the history of silver souvenir spoons, which originated in Europe, and which took off in popularity in the U.S. with the Salem Witch Spoon. In 1891, the Salem Witch Spoon was trademarked and sold seven thousand copies. It led to an explosion in the hobby of collecting souvenir spoons.

Cleo acted as the perfect assistant, putting the enlarged photos that I'd affixed to posterboard on the easel with just the right amount of flair. Anyone would think I'd brought her along to help me, not to make me feel safer.

I pointed to the last photo. "Here we see Claudius Grove, the railroad baron who funded the building of Grove College, at the ceremonial ribbon cutting, along with my own great-great-grandmother, Elsie Dorsett, who was the mayor of the town then. Doesn't the donor look proud to have a college named for him?"

"I've read several letters written by Elsie about the day." I continued. "She described how delighted Mr. Grove was with the three red-brick buildings next to a classic college green and how happy she was that she'd been able to encourage him to put this key component in place in the community she was trying to build. But from what she wrote, it wasn't only the two of them who were excited about the new college. The whole town was proud of the prestige and distinction that came from being home to an institution of higher learning."

Jessica blinked. "Your great-great-grandmother was the mayor?"

"She was. It makes my job so much more meaningful." I instinctively ran a hand down my pearls, which had belonged to Elsie.

Tabitha held up the Grove College spoon. "Is this very valuable?"

"Not terribly. The enamel shows some wear, and there are a few dings on the bowl. I'd say it's worth $25. But I think it shows what an important event the opening of Grove College was in the history of Dogwood Springs. We think of the town's economy today as mostly driven by tourism, but the college meant that boarding houses, a bookstore, and other businesses sprang up to support the student population."

I stopped there, conscious of the fact that my talks were supposed to be short. I wanted people to find history interesting and important, but I always had to watch myself so I didn't overdo it.

The alumni asked a few more questions, then seemed happy with the presentation, stood, and wandered out of the room. I had hoped I might catch Chad, but he slipped away while I was answering a final question from Kate. She thanked me again for coming out and suggested I leave my easel in the corner of the dining room. Then she headed upstairs, where she said she planned to download a good e-book to read about history, something to take her mind off Francie's death.

All in all, given the situation, I thought the presentation had gone well. But I was also here to investigate that death. I needed to talk to—

"Look." Cleo stood near the large dining room window at the side of the house and pointed. "Chad's just sitting there in the sunshine in the picnic area near the barn."

"Excellent!" I re-wrapped the souvenir spoon and slid it back into my purse. "Let's go talk to him."

We put the day's enlarged photos back in the car and approached Chad from behind, giving us a chance to observe him. His time as quarterback of the Grove University team might have been twenty-five years ago, but his shoulders still looked broad and his biceps strong.

Had he used that strength to bludgeon his wife before he ran over her with the tractor?

I shuddered, then drew in a deep breath. Someone needed to solve this crime and, while the sheriff seemed like he was trying, I didn't have that much confidence in him.

"Hey, Chad," I said softly.

He turned around.

"I wanted to tell you how sorry I am that Francie died," I said.

"Thanks." He shoved his hands in his pockets. "That, uh, that was a good talk. I'm not much into collecting stuff, but I liked the part about the Salem Witch Spoon. I've always been fascinated by those trials and the connection between them and how women were viewed by society at the time. Not a lot of men were tried as witches, you know?"

"It's a fascinating connection." And an observation that made me think more highly of him and hesitant to consider him a killer. Still, I was interested in that tension Hannah had sensed between him and Francie. But how to bring it up casually?

Bella sat beside me, head tilted as she looked at Chad.

I gazed off to the side, then turned back. "Losing

someone is so hard. No matter what, it feels like there are things that were left unsaid, emotions that were never conveyed." I crossed my fingers behind my back. Maybe that comment would spur him to say something that might give me some insight.

I'd barely gotten the words out when he looked directly at me. "That's so true. Until you've lived it, you don't think about that aspect of death. At least I didn't." Lines tightened around his eyes. "Take Francie and me. We were going through a rough patch."

I kept my face interested but neutral. No reason to give away that we were finally getting to the topic I wanted to discuss. Or that I was delighted he'd brought it up.

"I loved her, and I know she loved me. We'd been arguing more lately, but I knew we'd get through it. I secretly thought this week would remind her of when we were in college and rekindle our romance." He shook his head.

Was that action an expression of grief? Or a subconscious indication that his grief was a lie?

Chad pointed behind him with his thumb. "We had our first kiss under one of those apple trees. Not that it matters now, with her gone. So, I probably sound stupid."

"It doesn't sound stupid at all," Cleo said. "I could see how being where you fell in love could help a relationship get back on track."

"Thanks." His voice wobbled a little.

I glanced at Cleo. If anyone would understand about rekindling a romance, it was her. After more than a decade apart, she was happily dating Bryce, the guy she'd fallen in love with while they were in high school.

Maybe that was exactly what Chad had been hoping for when he came to the orchard. Were we wrong to suspect him? He could simply be a man who'd argued with his wife and who was now mourning her death, perhaps wracked with guilt that some of their last interactions had been difficult. Maybe I should look at things from a different angle.

I paused a moment, then continued. "I know you think it might have been the trespasser, but logically, it makes sense to consider other options. I mean, for all we know, the trespasser could be someone down on his luck who was hungry and took some apples."

Chad shrugged. "Yeah, I know I have to accept that it might have been one of our college friends."

"Had Francie spent a lot of time with any of them lately?"

"I can't imagine any reason one of them would have wanted to kill her. Believe me, I've tried to think." He scratched his head. "As for spending time together, the only thing I can think of is that she talked with Tabitha recently."

"Oh?"

"Tabitha applied for a job at Channel 7, but she didn't get it. And there was something off about the situation. I can't really explain it, but Francie acted odd. I think she felt bad that she couldn't help Tabitha get the position."

"Nothing else?" Cleo asked.

"Nothing. If I knew who killed her, I'd call the sheriff

right now. But I don't." Chad exhaled, and his shoulders slumped.

I glanced over at Cleo.

She angled her head toward my car.

"Thanks for talking with us, Chad. Again, my condolences."

He didn't even look up, not even when Bella walked over to him.

I called her over to me, and we headed to my car with Cleo.

After we were inside, I stashed my purse in the back and started the engine. "Well, that was interesting."

"Especially what Chad said about Tabitha," Cleo agreed.

"It's not a great lead, but it's all we've got. I think we need more information from someone who works at Channel 7 like ..." I grinned at Cleo.

"Sam's friend, Victor Dyer!" She pulled her phone from her purse and began typing. "I'm texting Sam to tell him what we learned. I'll have him contact Victor and see if he knows anything about Tabitha's application to Channel 7."

The message *whooshed* out.

"Excellent," I pulled onto Orchard Road. "We're already making progress in solving this murder."

Chapter Six

ONCE WE GOT BACK into town, I dropped Cleo and Bella at home and hurried to work. An hour later, I gave a tour of the building to Maureen, an older woman who was new to both the museum and to Dogwood Springs. We ended up in the gift shop, where Valerie Johnson, a woman in her mid-fifties who was one of our best volunteers, was straightening the shelves. As I'd come to expect, Valerie was wearing her favorite color, hyacinth blue, and was ready with a wide smile.

I introduced the two women, and they both said hello.

"This all looks great." Maureen turned to me. "I have so many questions about how to get started."

My phone dinged with a text. "Sorry, I should check this." I pulled it out of my pocket.

Sam Collins
Are you busy or can I call? I've got big news.

I stared down at the screen, desperate to hear his news. But I couldn't very well abandon Maureen when she had questions. And I wanted to get her started with some simple task today so she'd feel more invested and want to come back.

Valerie touched my shoulder. "Libby, if Maureen could stay with me a while, I could use her help. And I might be able to answer her questions while we worked."

Maureen's eyes lit. "I'd love to help."

"That would be great." I beamed at Valerie. Valerie had joined the museum's volunteer team a few months ago, had caught on quickly to every task we'd asked her to do, and had the patience to be a good teacher.

"You're going to love volunteering here," she said to Maureen as she repositioned her glasses. "It's been a great way for me to make friends in Dogwood Springs."

Valerie was so upbeat. No one would ever guess that the community where she'd previously lived in California had been destroyed by fire or that, soon after she moved here, her husband had died of a heart attack. If volunteering at the museum had helped her make friends, I couldn't be happier.

I gave them a quick wave, then ran back upstairs and called Sam.

He answered on the first ring. "Remember how Hannah

told us Francie and Tabitha were best friends in college?" he asked.

"Yeah."

"Well, I think I know why Francie acted odd about when Tabitha applied to work at Channel 7. Guilt."

Ooh. "Guilt?" This sounded promising.

"She's the reason Tabitha didn't get the job," Sam said. "The station manager was really impressed with Tabitha's application. I guess she's known in the business as quite a gem. Great on camera, loved by viewers, and a positive force in the newsroom. She only stayed in Omaha because that's where her ex-husband lives, and they shared custody of their kids. Her youngest is in college now, so she felt it was time to try for a bigger market."

"But she didn't get the job. What did Francie do?"

"She had enough sway to convince the station to go with the other top candidate, a woman who's much younger and less experienced."

"Wow. You'd think she'd have loved the chance to work with her friend."

"I know. Victor couldn't believe the station didn't snap Tabitha up. He's not sure how Francie convinced management to go with the younger woman."

"Why would she do that?"

"Victor didn't know for sure, but he thinks maybe Francie didn't want to lose her spot as the queen bee. Victor said Francie worked her butt off and broke big stories. But she wasn't that well-liked at the station. She might even have thought they were going to hire Tabitha, then let her go."

"Did Victor think Tabitha knew that Francie kept her from getting the job?"

"He said he wouldn't be surprised. His words, not mine, but apparently reporters like to gossip."

I didn't know much about journalism, but I did know that broadcasters always wanted to move up to bigger viewing audiences. Tabitha had stayed in Omaha for her kids but now had a chance to seek more success. And the St. Louis metro area had to be more than double the size of Omaha. "So, Tabitha may have had two reasons to kill Francie. She'd betrayed their friendship, and she'd sabotaged her chance to land a good job."

"Looks like it," Sam said.

"Well then, tomorrow when I go back to the orchard, I need to talk to Tabitha."

I hung up and thought for a moment. Then I called Kate and asked if she had been happy with my presentation about the spoon. She had been. So, I casually asked if the timing of the talks was working out well. Were the alums having to get up early on account of me?

"Only Jessica." Kate chuckled. "Most of us get up fairly early, and Tabitha's a real early bird. By the time I get up at seven, she's almost always in the kitchen baking something. I think you're coming at the perfect time."

I thanked her, hung up, and sent a text to Alice, who I knew was also an early riser, to see if she could go with me.

She readily agreed, and we made plans to try to see Tabitha before my next talk.

That evening, after I reviewed my presentation for the next morning, I decided to bake peanut butter cookies to take to work for Rodney's birthday. It was an easy recipe, and soon I had forty cookies, neatly lined up on waxed paper, cooling on my kitchen counter.

A photo would be perfect. I could send it to Imani to let her know my plan. I dashed into the living room to get my phone. But then I got all caught up reading a text from Sam, who'd unexpectedly messaged to tell me he loved me.

My heart melted a little and I looked up as Bella walked in from the kitchen. "Aww, Bella, isn't he wonderful?"

She gave a happy doggy smile and thumped her tail as if to remind me that she thoroughly approved of Sam.

I went back into the kitchen, ready to take my photo.

Except ... three cookies had mysteriously disappeared.

"Bella!" No wonder she had looked so happy. "You know you're not supposed to get on the counter."

She hung her head, then snuck a peek at me.

I gave her a stern look. Which wasn't easy. She was just so cute.

But golden retrievers had a tendency to eat things they shouldn't. I had to be firm.

I looked back at the cookies that were left. A few near

the edge had been moved out of their neat rows. I wouldn't be taking those to Rodney. Or eating them myself.

Luckily, most of them had been out of her reach. I scooted the ones I was sure had escaped doggy drool farther back and kept an eye on Bella until they were cool enough to wrap for tomorrow.

And, after I explained in detail to Bella that getting on the counter was wrong, I scratched behind her ears and told her that I loved her.

After all, peanut butter cookies were hard to resist. I should have been more careful.

I texted Sam back, told him about Bella's cookie snack, and sent him a long string of heart emojis.

The next morning, Alice met Bella and me at the orchard half an hour before my scheduled presentation time. For the day's talk, I'd brought the original business ledger of a local shoe factory from the 1930s as well as large photos of several key pages to display on the easel.

No one answered when we knocked, but I wasn't expected for a while, and most of the alums were probably upstairs brushing their teeth after breakfast and getting ready for the day.

The front door of the retreat center was open, so Alice, Bella, and I went in.

While we were setting up things in the dining room, I heard Deputy Miller, who must have lucked out with daytime duty all week, talking on the phone. I tapped Alice's arm and laid a finger over my lips.

"Yes, sir," Deputy Miller said. "Yesterday afternoon, I searched more rows of the orchard, and I found clearer footprints matching those at the crime scene."

I shot a glance at Alice. The deputies were doing more than I'd thought.

"Yeah," the deputy said. "I took photos of them in both places and made two plaster casts. If we come up with a suspect, we should have a way to tie them to the murder site."

Footsteps echoed down the tile floor in the hall. "Thank you, sir," Deputy Miller said.

The front door opened, footsteps left the hall and went outside, and the door closed.

"Goodness!" Alice whispered.

"I wish we could hear the rest," I whispered back in case he was on the porch. "But I imagine he'd notice if we walked outside and hung around next to him."

"Time to talk to Tabitha, then," Alice mouthed.

I nodded.

We peeked through the doorway into the kitchen.

The room was large, bright, and sunny, with two big windows on one wall and a third over the sink. A wooden worktable filled the center of the room and, by the two windows where one might put a kitchen table, a blue-and-white gingham couch encouraged people to sit and chat with the cook. Something was already baking in the oven, and I caught the scent of what I thought might be homemade bread.

Tabitha stood behind a wooden worktable, oblivious to us thanks to whatever she was listening to through her earbuds. Her ash-blond hair was pulled back in a ponytail, and her face held a look of contentment as she took all the peel off an apple in one long, thin, continuous curl.

Alice and I caught her attention as we walked to the other side of the table.

She pulled out her earbuds. "Good morning! Am I late for today's presentation?" She glanced at the clock on the stove.

"No, we're early." I introduced Alice, mentioning that she was a key volunteer at the museum here to help with my presentation.

Bella walked over to Tabitha, looking up hopefully, but seemed to understand she was cooking and lay down in a sunbeam near a window.

"In spite of what's happened, you look happy in here," I said.

Tabitha's eyes clouded, and she set down her knife on the apple-shaped chopping board that Hannah had mentioned. Now that I saw it, I recognized the skilled craftsmanship of Dale Jones, Imani's husband.

"I really am sad about Francie." Tabitha gestured awkwardly. "But baking always perks me up. I just love creating something that I know people will enjoy."

"I understand," Alice said. "I like to bake too."

"I guess even after the tragedy, the kitchen is where I feel most comfortable." Tabitha set down the apple she'd peeled. "Since we're stuck at the retreat center, we've each kind of found a spot to call our own. Kate hangs out in the living room. Derek on the back porch. Jessica wanders around in the orchard, and Chad seems to like the picnic area. Hannah and Noah have their own house, of course, and the farm market out by the road. For me, it's the kitchen."

"That makes sense," I said. "You'd expect unease after the murder. People would want their own space."

"Yeah," Tabitha said.

I took a half step forward. Time to drop my little bombshell. "It has to be especially awkward for you. After all, Francie sabotaged your application to work at Channel 7 in St. Louis."

Shock followed by pain flashed through Tabitha's eyes. "She did? How do you know that?"

"That's what Victor Dyer says," I said.

Tabitha blinked rapidly and pressed her fist against her mouth. Then her eyes narrowed and grew harder. "And you're telling me this—why? To see if you can judge by my reaction if I killed her? I heard the sheriff say you were an amateur detective."

A ripple of apprehension shot through me, my gaze flicking to the glint of the paring knife inches away from her hands.

"Libby's worked a lot with the local police." Alice's voice held a note of warning, as if she, too, was uncomfortable with that knife. "She's solved several murders that the local police couldn't."

I gave a small shrug, trying to look calm. "And I hate to admit it, but I don't have much faith in Billy Harper."

Tabitha's lips pursed up, and she stared at me, jaw tight.

I kept silent. Sometimes, if you were quiet, people divulged more than they intended.

Seconds ticked by.

Just when I thought I couldn't keep quiet any longer, Tabitha's face eased. "I guess I sort of understand. I don't have much faith in the sheriff either." She glanced down and shifted her weight. "The answer to your question is no, I didn't know what Francie had done. I simply thought I didn't make the cut. So, I didn't have a reason to kill her."

She looked off to one side, then returned her gaze to us. "I'll have to get in touch with someone I know at Channel 7. He's just a casual acquaintance, but I need to find out more about what happened."

"That's a good idea," I said. Although it might not be information she wanted to hear.

She let out a sigh. "Really, I know Francie. I should have realized she would feel threatened if I applied at her station, but I honestly thought it would be fun to work together." She tipped her head to one side. "I guess I shouldn't be so upset with you for asking questions. I've certainly asked enough of them in my line of work."

I smoothed my hair. She probably had. She'd probably even dropped some bombshells of her own on people she was interviewing.

"Maybe if you figure out who killed Francie, the sheriff will let us go home." She gave an exaggerated shudder. "I hate staying here, barely able to sleep at night because I'm so nervous."

"I would think if the murderer is caught, you'll be free to leave," Alice said.

"Would you be willing to help us then?" I asked. "Like tell us if you've noticed anything suspicious? Or overheard a conversation between Francie and someone else that didn't seem important but later stuck in your mind?"

"None of that." Tabitha picked up the knife, chopped the apple in quarters, and cored each section. "I ..." She shook her head. "No, I shouldn't."

"If you know something, please tell us," I said.

Tabitha lowered her voice. "I do know someone who had a reason to hate Francie, but they'd never in a million years do anything about it."

"Who?" Alice and I said in unison.

Tabitha cut the apple section into thin, equal slices. "I'll tell you, but take this as a reflection of Francie's character, not an accusation. It's information to help you understand who Francie was so you can solve this."

"Okay. Who are you referring to?"

"Jessica."

I blinked. I hadn't expected her to say that.

"Back in college, Francie was horrid to Jessica. I tried to get her to stop, but it was almost like she couldn't keep herself from making nasty comments and putting Jessica down. Jessica was so sensitive that those comments just crushed her. I didn't hear Francie say anything after we got here for the reunion, but there was something in the way she looked at Jessica that made me think she was going to start all over again."

I exchanged glances with Alice. "That seems sort of iffy. I mean, Francie was a grown woman. Too old to act like a catty eighth grader."

Tabitha dipped her chin and gave me a dubious look. "Are you forgetting what you just told me about Channel 7?"

"Oh." She was right. And Jessica had been subdued, even before Francie was killed. Maybe she hadn't been nervous about meeting me like I'd thought. Maybe she'd been angry with Francie, possibly holding a grudge from back in college that had been compounded by more recent cruel comments.

"Like I said, Jessica has a reason to hate Francie, even if only from what she endured twenty-five years ago, but she would never do anything about it. She's too nice and ... well, she'd never have the guts."

Footsteps echoed from the hall as some of the other alums came downstairs.

"Even so," I said, "after I give my presentation, I think I should talk with her."

"Well, don't tell her I said anything." Tabitha began slicing the next section of apple.

"I won't mention your name, I promise." Maybe Tabitha was right, and Jessica was too meek to commit a murder.

But after my presentation, I was definitely talking to her.

Chapter Seven

A FEW MINUTES LATER, after I'd stopped in the bathroom to wash my hands, the alumni were back in their same seats around the dining room table.

Bella went from person to person, tilting her head in that heart-melting way that invited ear rubs, resting her head on their knees, or simply standing and gazing at them with love as they told her what a beautiful, very good girl she was.

After she made the rounds, she returned to Chad and nudged his hand.

His dull eyes lit, and he stroked her neck until she lay down beside him.

My heart warmed just watching her. She was such a sweet dog, so caring and intuitive about when people were in pain. Maybe that was part of the reason she'd been so good for me when I'd first moved to Dogwood Springs.

Maybe she had sensed that I needed her as much as she needed me.

Beside me, Alice flipped through the enlarged images I'd made of the shoe factory ledger, ready to put them on the easel when I cued her.

I gave Bella one last look, then introduced Alice to the group and began the day's presentation.

"Today, I brought with me the ledger from the Roberts Shoe Factory, which used to stand between Third and Fourth Streets, two blocks west of Main." I held up the ledger and opened it to the first page I'd enlarged.

Derek shifted in his seat, his face tense, then muttered under his breath to Jessica.

Now she looked uncomfortable too.

"Is everything okay?" I asked.

"Forgive me for interjecting," he said, "but isn't it standard practice to use gloves while examining historical texts?"

Ahh, that explained it. "That's a common misconception. Sometimes gloves are required if the book is moldy, or if it contains photographs or is decorated with metal or ivory. In general, though, the best thing to do is to wash your hands first and dry them thoroughly, which I did right before we began."

There was a murmur of surprise at the table.

"Gloves reduce a person's sense of touch," I explained, "which can lead to tears or other damage to a book." I gestured to the first enlargement, which Alice had slid into place. "And to reduce the possibility of any damage, I'm not actually going to pass the ledger around. I've got enlargements of the key pages I'll be discussing. But I did want you to see the real artifact."

Derek sat back with a visible look of relief.

"I'm passionate about making history accessible to everyone," I said. "But I do sometimes wish all the visitors to the museum were as concerned about the artifacts as you are."

I exchanged glances with Alice. As she knew all too well in her position as president of the museum's board of directors, I could tell some tales about visitors who wanted to test the historic chairs to see if they were comfortable, to rearrange a display so they could take a selfie in the middle of it, or to give their kids sticky treats inside the museum's display areas despite the "No Food or Drink Allowed" sign.

But I wasn't here to discuss the challenges of running a museum. I gave my best professional smile and began my talk. "By 1914, partly thanks to its location by both the Mississippi River and railroads, St. Louis led the nation's shoe manufacturing industry. Much of the labor was done at affiliated businesses in small Missouri towns, including Dogwood Springs, then called Silersville."

I had Alice bring up the next image, a page from the local newspaper that showed some of the shoes made in the local business's first year of production, and I moved on to discuss how the shoe factory had been an important change for the area, the beginning of a shift from industries such as mining and lumber into manufacturing.

"The factory provided much-needed jobs, and for many

women, those positions were their first work outside the home. I know of one family who tragically lost their father to influenza. The mother stayed home with the younger children. The three older daughters, who had all finished high school, took jobs in the shoe factory." I pointed to an entry on the next image Alice displayed, one that showed the three women's names on the payroll. "Those jobs provided vital income, and with careful savings, the three young women were eventually able to follow their dream and open a dress shop here in town."

"I love that," Kate said.

The alumni all seemed interested in the shoe factory, and Hannah even contributed that her grandmother had worked there before she married. Eventually, after a lively discussion about the disparity between the wages of women and men at the time, I brought things to a close. Time had passed quickly, but I could smell Tabitha's apple pie from the kitchen. It was time to stop.

Afterward, the group all left at once, and Alice and I spotted Jessica wandering out into the orchard.

We slipped on our jackets and followed her to a hill where she sat on the ground with the sun on her shoulders, reading through a small notebook.

Right before we reached her, Alice sneezed.

Jessica startled and scrambled to her feet. "Libby, and ... Alice, is it?"

"You have a good memory," Alice said.

Jessica didn't seem to notice Bella, who sat down beside

me, and she ran a hand over the back of her neck. "Can I help you?"

"I'm still upset about Francie's murder." I zipped up my jacket. Jessica was in the sun, but in order to face her, I was in the shadow of one of the apple trees. "The facts keep running through my head like a puzzle I can't solve."

"I wish the sheriff would figure it out," Jessica said. "At this point, I don't have any desire to spend time around the people I hung out with in college, not if one of them is a murderer."

Odd. She didn't call them friends—just people she hung out with. That simple word choice spoke volumes.

"Is there anything you might have noticed? Someone who seemed upset with Francie after you all got here?" Alice asked.

"No." Jessica picked at the side seam of her jeans. "I can't think of anything."

"Any issues that might have lingered from when you were in college?" I asked. "I don't mean to speak ill of the dead, but I get the impression that Francie didn't always consider the feelings of other people. I even heard she was rude to you, maybe even rude enough to ..." I made an awkward gesture with my hands.

Jessica's cheeks turned bright red. "That's true, but I never, I couldn't, I mean—"

"She means," Derek said sharply as he appeared from over a small ridge, "that she couldn't have been the person who killed Francie, no matter what you're implying."

I stepped back, surprised by his tone.

Bella, who also seemed startled, let out a soft growl.

But Jessica's eyes lit as she turned to him.

"Jessica was with me, picking apples, when Francie died," Derek said, his tone now measured. "I explained that to the sheriff when he interviewed me."

"Oh." I ran a hand over my collarbone and edged back. If only the sheriff had stayed at the picnic tables instead of moving his interviews to the porch of the old farmhouse, I'd have heard that conversation.

"We all share a vested interest in resolving this situation expeditiously," Derek added, "but I can assure you, the perpetrator is not Jessica."

I glanced over at Alice. It did seem like we were on the wrong track. "That makes sense. If the two of you were together, you're both in the clear. But someone killed Francie." I looked at Jessica, then at Derek. "Did either of you notice anything suspicious the day of the murder? Or later on?"

"No. Nothing," Derek said. But he pressed his hand against his mouth as if he was holding in a secret.

Maybe I wasn't asking the right question. "Is there someone you think might have a motive for killing Francie?"

He pressed his lips together, then let his breath out in a *whoosh*. "It pains me to suggest this, but if I were tasked with identifying Francie's assailant, my investigation would likely focus on Kate."

"Kate?" She'd been nothing but kind and always so supportive of the museum.

"She was the individual who discovered the body, which, as we know, is frequently a line of inquiry law enforcement finds prudent to follow," he said. "The scenario of committing the act and then posing as the finder is not uncommon."

I hadn't thought of that.

"I don't recall any specific issues between her and Francie in college," Derek added. "However, Francie's reputation for investigative reporting could certainly have posed a significant threat to a business owner like Kate, should she have unearthed something damaging."

"True." I had trouble seeing Kate as a killer, but he made a valid point.

"You know ..." Jessica crossed one arm over her chest and propped her chin on her other fist, her eyes narrowed. "Kate was also the person who arranged for us to come into town early for the reunion and stay here at the orchard. I guess she could have done that on purpose, so she could have the opportunity to kill Francie."

"An excellent observation," Derek said, his tone one he might have used in the classroom when commending a student who'd made a particularly astute comment. "And we all heard that the killer wore Noah's gloves when they drove the tractor. Kate might have entered the barn and taken them."

Yes, she could have. I'd been so busy thinking about my presentation that first evening at the orchard that I wouldn't have noticed. "You've given us a lot to think about. Thanks for your time. I'm—" I reached out to touch Jessica's sleeve — "I'm sorry I suspected you."

Bella, Alice, and I went back to the retreat center, collected the supplies we'd brought, and walked to our cars. My mind was swirling the whole way.

Kate *had* looked at Francie with disapproval when she introduced us.

And I had to admit that no matter how nice Kate was, in the end, she'd gotten what she'd wanted. Look at how she'd convinced me to do the series of talks.

Plus, Derek could be right. Francie could have uncovered something that Kate was determined to keep secret. "I guess we can't ignore Kate as a suspect just because she contributes so heavily to the museum."

"No, we can't," Alice agreed. "And if Derek and Jessica were together at the time of the murder, there are only four possible suspects remaining."

I nodded. "Chad, who no matter what he says, may have killed Francie because of problems in their marriage. Kate, who might have wanted to stop Francie from divulging something that could damage her real estate business. Tabitha, who could just be a really good actress and may have actually known that Francie sabotaged her job application and taken her revenge."

"And the trespasser," Alice added. "But we have no way of knowing who that is or what their motive might be."

I straightened my shoulders. "So, we need to thoroughly investigate Chad, Tabitha, and—as awkward as it may be—Kate."

Chapter Eight

I TOOK BELLA HOME, let her out in the backyard for a few minutes, and made sure she had plenty of fresh water.

While she was outside, I got a text from my landlord. The plumber could come by tomorrow to fix my leaky faucet, but Bella would have to be out of the unit. Apparently, he had dealt with pet-related issues in the past and would only come if Bella was gone.

I turned off my phone, let Bella back in, and ran a hand over her soft fur. Sometimes, when the museum was closed, I took her in with me to keep me company in my office while I worked. But all day was too long for her to sit quietly in my office, and I didn't want to explain to museum visitors why they heard a dog barking upstairs. I sent an email to Sam and Alice. Could either of them possibly help me out?

Alice replied to say she unfortunately couldn't help. But

she did volunteer Doug to go with me to talk to Kate the next morning.

A half-second later, I got a reply from Sam. He wasn't teaching the next day and could easily take his meetings in video calls. He sounded almost excited at the prospect of having Bella visit.

I quickly thanked him, then texted my landlord to say tomorrow would work well and told Bella the plan.

I grabbed the peanut butter cookies I'd packed, took them in, and placed them on the table in the museum conference room for the staff and volunteers to share. Rodney was delighted, and everyone told me they were delicious.

I refrained from telling them that Bella agreed.

By ten, I was at my desk, looking over the schedule of school tours Imani had planned for the rest of the month. What with classes coming into the museum from Dogwood Springs and several surrounding towns, October was going to be busy.

Somehow, in all the excitement of getting ready to talk to Tabitha and planning for Bella tomorrow, I had forgotten to pack my lunch. Normally, if I packed something the night before and ate at my desk, I had time to go home to let Bella out. When Rodney said he was going to Miller's Sub Shop and asked if I wanted him to bring me back a sandwich, I gratefully accepted. Half an hour later, after dashing home to Bella, I was nibbling at a spicy Italian sub as I answered email at my desk.

I had just taken a bite when I heard footsteps coming toward my office, and Sam appeared in my doorway.

A swirl of happiness wrapped around my heart. What a nice surprise! I wiped my mouth and set my sandwich aside. "Well, hello! What brings you by?"

"I don't mean to interrupt your lunch."

I waved a dismissive hand at my food. "What's going on? Is there a problem with keeping Bella tomorrow?"

"No, no problem with Bella." He slid into the chair across from my desk. "You're probably focused on the murder out at the orchard, but ..."

"Yes, but you sound like you know something interesting. What's up?"

"I was downtown as part of a group taking a faculty candidate out to lunch, and I got a call from the owner of that antique shop, Yesterday's Treasures. She's back in town."

My pulse picked up.

A couple of months ago, Sam had discovered two secret compartments in an antique bookcase that his interior designer had chosen for his front hall. We found that one of the secret compartments contained a sealed letter. It was written in the 1960s from a dying mother to her daughter, explaining that her life had all been a lie. She'd encouraged her daughter to read the diary she'd hidden in the fireplace to learn the truth.

Sam and I had realized that if the letter was still unopened, the diary had probably never been found. We'd been intrigued but clueless as to where to look for the fireplace, and the antique dealer who sold the bookcase to the designer couldn't be reached.

"Did the antique dealer know where she got that book-case? And did she say why she took so long to return your call?"

"She was on a buying trip and had some medical problems. She said she's all better, though, and she knows exactly where the bookcase came from." His eyes twinkled as if he was enjoying keeping me in suspense.

"Well?" I gestured for him to hurry up and tell me.

"The dealer bought it at the estate sale of Ester Daniels when she was moving to an assisted-living facility here in town. And ..." Sam paused dramatically and grinned at me.

"And?" I said eagerly.

"And I called Ester, and she'd be delighted to have us visit this evening about seven."

"Yes!" I jumped out of my chair, ran around my desk, and hugged Sam. "That's excellent news! If she's the daughter of the woman who hid the letter, she can tell us where her mom lived, we can ask the current owners to let us retrieve the diary, and then Ester can read it and learn what her mom wanted to tell her."

"And maybe she'll tell us her mom's big secret. Ever since I read that old letter, I've been dying to know."

"I sure hope she will," I agreed. "Even if she keeps it private, though, the woman who wrote that letter wanted her family to know the truth. That's what really matters."

Sam gave a reluctant nod, pulled out his phone, and

checked the time. "I guess I better head back to campus. I've got a class soon, and parking midday is a mess."

We agreed that he would pick me up at six, we'd grab a quick dinner at my favorite Mexican restaurant, and then we'd go visit Ester.

He kissed me goodbye and dashed out the door.

I sat back in my chair, ate another bite of my sandwich, and wondered where that diary might be hidden. Of course, figuring out who killed Francie was the priority, but Doug and I would talk with Kate in the morning. In the meantime, I was ready for some historical sleuthing.

Ester lived in a retirement complex called Tranquility Hills, which had three options—one-story independent-living condos, a large assisted-living building, and a skilled nursing facility. Ester was in the assisted-living building, which meant we turned right as we entered Tranquility Hills.

Neither Sam nor I had ever been to the complex, which was located northwest of town, and as we approached it after dinner, we were both impressed. From the size of the trees, it looked like it had been built about ten years ago. The grounds were beautifully landscaped and had a park-like feel. Inside, the assisted-living building was so clean it sparkled. A big-band classic from the 1940s played softly over the sound system, and in a room near the lobby, a speaker lectured a group of about twenty people on the geology of the Dogwood Springs area. The delicious aromas of freshly baked bread and roast beef filled the air. A woman at the front desk smiled and asked who we were visiting.

A few minutes later, we knocked on the door of Apartment 137.

"Welcome!" A white-haired woman gestured for us to come inside and silenced the classical music she'd been playing. "I'm Ester, and I'm so interested to hear about this mystery you've found."

Sam and I introduced ourselves, and Ester led us to her living room and waved us toward a bright-red leather couch. A bold modern painting hung above the couch, and a narrow cabinet displayed vivid ceramic pieces.

"What a great painting." Sam gazed up at it. "Who's the artist?"

Ester's face lit as she sat in an armchair across from us. "Me!"

He gestured to a tall vase. "And the ceramics?"

"Me as well." Her face beamed. "I've painted for years, but I never did ceramics before I moved in here. I have to admit, the studio was one of the things that attracted me to Tranquility Hills. It has all the supplies and equipment we need, and our instructor also teaches at Grove University. I'm learning so much."

"Wow." I loved the fact that she was still creating art and that Tranquility Hills was supporting such an active, vibrant lifestyle.

"Enough about me." Ester settled back in her chair. "Tell me about this mystery."

"When you had your estate sale, your antique bookcase was bought by the woman who owns the Yesterday's Treasures antique shop out south of town," I said.

"I heard that," Ester said. "I didn't attend the sale. People told me it would make me mad if something I thought was valuable went for a steal."

"That sounds smart." No need to make the transition to a new situation more difficult. "Sam's been working with an interior designer who's still adding touches to his house. She bought that bookcase for his front hall."

Sam leaned back into the couch. "She told me about the hidden compartments in the base—"

"The liquor cubbies!" Ester said with a laugh.

"That's what she called them too," Sam said. "I thought those were the only secrets in the bookcase, but a couple of months ago, I noticed a place where the wood around one of the shelves on the side was thicker than the others. That side shelf was actually a box with an open side where the books went. The box could be removed and a second, secret box sat behind it."

Ester raised a hand to her chest. "Imagine that. I never even knew."

"The first compartment Sam checked was empty, but we found a matching secret box on the other side of the bookcase, and inside it, we found a letter. We think it might have been from your mom."

Sam held the letter toward her. "I hope you don't mind that we opened it. We didn't know what it was at first."

Ester took the letter, adjusted her glasses, and turned on a reading lamp beside her chair. "I doubt it was written to me, but I can't resist reading it."

Sam and I exchanged glances while she peered down at the letter.

"Oh, my." Ester looked up at us. "This must have been written to my dear friend, Doris Atkins. She gave the book-case to me when she cleaned out her mother's house after she died."

"Do you know how we can contact her?" Sam asked.

Ester shook her head. "Doris has been dead for at least twenty years. She had a daughter, but I've no idea where she is."

"So, the fireplace where the diary was hidden would be in the house where Doris's mother lived in the 1960s?" I asked.

"Yes," Ester said. "It was over on Rosewood Street. A yellow house with a big covered front porch. I think you'd call it Craftsman style, but I don't even know if it's still there. The university's been buying up property near there and expanding."

Oh, I'd be crushed if the house had been torn down and the diary destroyed. "What was Doris's mother's name?"

"The last name was Riley." Ester's eyes narrowed, and she pressed a hand against her chin for a moment. "Hattie Riley," she said with a note of triumph.

"I wonder why Doris didn't look in the secret compartment," Sam said. "Her mother seemed so sure she would."

"Doris was really broken up about her mom's death. She may have been too caught up in her grief to think of it. And at the time, she was quite busy running a business in California and raising her daughter. I remember her saying that her mother loved the bookcase but that she didn't have room for it in her house.

Sam turned to me. "Even if we can't get the letter to the intended recipient, I still want to know what Doris's secret was, don't you?"

I nodded emphatically. "How about we drive over to Rosewood Street and see if the yellow house is still there? If it is, it may still have the diary hidden in the fireplace."

"If you find the yellow house, let me know." Ester's eyes gleamed. "This is so exciting. I can't wait to hear what you discover."

Sam and I chatted a bit more with Ester, learning more about her artwork, and I got her cell number. Then we hurried out to Sam's car.

"Do you know where Rosewood Street is?" I asked as I climbed in.

"Yep. I've seen a sign for it near campus." Sam started his engine, and about fifteen minutes later, we turned onto the street.

At first, all we saw were university offices on one side and a vacant lot, fenced off for construction on the other side.

My heart sank, and I looked over at Sam. "What if it's been torn down?"

"Don't give up yet. It looks like the road curves ahead." He rounded the bend.

"There!" I pointed at a large, two-story yellow house with a sprawling front porch. "That has to be it. Craftsman style and everything."

Sam grinned at me. "That's it—the house that may have the diary hidden in the fireplace."

"It's only eight fifteen. Do you think we could just knock and ask about the fireplace?"

Sam was already out of the car, coming around to open my door. "No harm in trying."

We climbed the wooden steps to the porch, and I knocked on the door.

But there was no answer. And although the house was close to campus, the neighborhood was so quiet that all I heard was the rustle of some small creature scurrying through the leaves.

"They're probably out for the evening," Sam said.

"What if they're out of town? They don't have a pumpkin on their porch."

"Well, neither do you, yet. Besides, not everyone decorates for Halloween. Maybe there aren't many kids in this neighborhood."

"You're right. We've got the address—38 Rosewood—so we can probably find their name and phone number online."

"Easily," Sam said.

Dating a tech whiz definitely had its advantages.

I texted Ester again and told her we were stalled for now but promised to keep her updated.

Sam walked with me back to his car. "I've got three flavors of Minnesota's Pride ice cream in my freezer, including that new peach cheesecake one you liked so much."

Why was I not surprised? Sam loved ice cream, especially Minnesota's Pride.

"Would you like to pick up Bella and come out to my house for a while?" he asked.

I glanced at the clock on the dashboard. "I promised myself I'd practice my talk for tomorrow morning. I know a certain golden retriever who will be a very attentive audience." I touched his arm. "Can I have a rain check?"

"Sure." He started the engine. "You're bringing Bella by tomorrow morning?"

"Mid-morning. After we've been to the orchard. If you're sure it's not too much trouble."

"No trouble at all. If the plumber asks that there be no pets in the unit at the time of the repair, she's got to go somewhere. And I'll mostly be grading. I'll get more done without the distraction of people stopping by my office."

"Thank you."

"Is Doug still going with you tomorrow?"

"He's meeting me at the orchard."

"Good. I'll feel better if you're not there alone."

Sam drove me back to my house and walked me to my

door. "You promise you'll be careful tomorrow, Libby?" He slid his arms around my waist.

"I promise." I gazed up at him, and warmth filled my chest. How had I gotten lucky enough to find a man who loved me so much?

He leaned down and brought his lips to mine.

Tingles shot through me, and we kissed until Bella barked from inside.

Breathless and a little dazed, I stepped back.

"I guess I need to let you practice your talk …" he said.

"I guess so."

"More kisses later?"

"Definitely." I caught one of his hands in mine, squeezed it, and went in.

Chapter Nine

THE NEXT MORNING, the sun was bright, but the air had a sharper nip in it. It must have felt perfect to Bella though. She trotted happily along on our Friday morning walk, while I kept wishing I'd brought my lightweight knit gloves.

It took me a little while to get packed up for the day, but as soon as I said the word *car*, she ran to the door, eager to leave.

When we arrived at the orchard, Doug was already parked in front of the retreat center. He walked over as I got out of my car. "Do you need anything carried in?"

"I'd love it if you'd get a box I have in my trunk." I let Bella out, waited while she greeted Doug, then popped the trunk open.

As Doug lifted the cardboard box, I leaned in closer. "Thanks for being here. I feel really uncomfortable about talking with Kate. I know leaving a killer unidentified could mean someone else might die, but I don't want to offend a major donor to the museum."

"No problem. Alice explained the whole situation. I'll help smooth things out if needed or ask the tough questions if you can't quite work the conversation around to them. And I'll keep my ears open for any other clues."

The tension in my shoulders eased. Doug ran a large company with hundreds of employees, and he frequently negotiated with suppliers. I was sure he'd handled lots of difficult conversations. Plus, he had a natural ease with people.

I got my purse and the enlarged photographs I'd brought out of the back seat.

Inside, I caught the sweet scent of what I thought was banana bread, and I heard water running upstairs. Some of the alums were still getting ready for the day.

I set my photos on the easel in the dining room and scattered items from the box across the table. Doug lingered in the hall with his head tilted slightly as if he were listening for conversations between the alums. Bella stood near the doorway, eager to greet each person as they came in.

"Pie pans?" Hannah said as she walked in and sat down.

"Very special pie pans," I said.

Each of the other alums wandered in, stopped to pet Bella, and took their regular seat at the table. Once they all arrived, Bella circled the table, getting additional attention, then went over beside Chad.

"Hello, girl," he said as he rubbed her ears.

She sat down next to him.

"Today," I began, "I want to talk with you about the beginnings of tourism in Dogwood Springs. Two key factors helped bring visitors to the area—the damming of rivers for hydroelectric power, which created lakes, like the Lake of the Ozarks, and the building of Route 66, which was completely paved in Missouri by 1931. Route 66 was advertised as 'the shortest, best, and most scenic route from Chicago through St. Louis to Los Angeles.'"

The alums nodded, all familiar with the famous highway.

"One of the businesses that sprung up to cater to those tourists was Mary's Fine Pies, run by Mary Smith." I held up one of the tin pie pans, and, as I'd asked him to, Doug put an enlarged photo of historic downtown Dogwood Springs on the easel. "Mary was a tiny woman, barely five feet tall, and was described as having curly blond hair and a heart of gold. From what I've read, she was widowed at an early age, then moved to Dogwood Springs. She worked at a local hotel for several years but eventually started her own shop."

I pointed to the photo on the easel. "Mary's Fine Pies stood on the site of what is now the Dogwood Café. Back when it first opened, it wasn't that common for a single woman to own a business. But like the three sisters I mentioned yesterday who had worked at the shoe factory and opened their own dress shop, she was determined."

"Good for her," Tabitha said.

I grinned. "Mary's restaurant became a mainstay of the

community, a popular place to stop to enjoy a slice of pie or take home an entire pie for a special evening. She made all the pies herself, and legend has it she never shared a single one of her recipes, not even after she retired."

"I know she must have done that for professional reasons," Derek said, "but I remember my grandmother had a recipe that had been given to her by a friend, who told her she could never share it. Quite a difference from today when home cooks share recipes all over the internet."

Excellent. I loved it when people could see connections to history in their own lives. "I haven't found any written accounts from Mary herself, but anecdotally, I've been told she was always ready to contribute to a worthy cause or to help someone in need. She saw Dogwood Springs as a place that offered her a second chance, and she wanted to pay that kindness forward."

"What a great story," Kate said.

I led the discussion to other aspects of early Missouri tourism, such as the system of restaurants, gas stations, bus terminals, and rest areas run by the Pierce Petroleum Corporation.

After another few minutes, I brought the presentation to an end and told them how nice it was to talk with people with such a deep interest in history.

Doug packed up the pie pans while I dealt with an urgent text from Imani with a question about scheduling school visits. Then he carried the pie pans out to my car along with the enlarged photos and the easel, which Imani needed at the museum over the weekend.

A few minutes later, he came back into the dining room. "Time to talk to Kate?"

I hit send on my text to Imani, grabbed my jacket, and gestured for Doug and Bella to follow me. We stepped into the hall, and I stuck my head in the doorway of the living room. As I'd expected, Kate was curled up in an upholstered chair with an e-reader on her lap.

"Well, hello, Libby. Hello, Doug." She set her e-reader aside. "What's up?"

I'd talked with Alice extensively, and we had agreed that the direct approach was best with Kate. If she was innocent, she'd understand my question. If not, well, she probably wasn't going to be making contributions to the museum from prison. But—though I had the support of the president of the museum's board of directors and her husband, Doug, by my side—this conversation made me nervous.

Standing here looking awkward, though, wasn't helping anything. "I'd like to talk with you for a moment if you don't mind."

Kate gestured to the couch across from her.

"It's ... rather delicate," I said, my voice faltering. "Could we walk outside?"

Kate's forehead furrowed, and she stood. "Sure. Just let me run upstairs and grab a jacket."

"Thanks." I glanced over at Doug, and he smiled encouragingly.

Kate returned to the living room, carrying a red plaid wool jacket. She slid it on and angled her head toward the front door. "Shall we?"

I put on my own jacket and followed her outside. The three of us walked partway down a path between two rows in the orchard where the apples had already been picked and stopped in a sunny spot.

In the distance, I heard Noah and Hannah discussing which row of apples to start picking, and Bella sniffed the air as if she picked up on something the rest of us didn't. Whatever it was, it wasn't a squirrel, or she would have been barking. Any squirrel within the vicinity was, in Bella's opinion, reason for sounding an emergency alert.

I drew in a deep breath. "This is horribly awkward, Kate, but Hannah is very concerned about the orchard. She's upset by Francie's death, of course, but she also came to me privately and told me she's worried that the tragedy here at the orchard will be awful for their business."

"I can only imagine," Kate said. "This has to be their best season."

"In the past, I've gotten involved in some odd things that went on in town. You may remember last spring when the wife of a major donor was poisoned at a reception at the museum."

Kate raised her eyebrows. "How could I forget hearing about that?"

"I've been able to help the police by finding a clue or two. Because of that, Hannah asked me to be on the lookout for anything unusual."

"Which is why you were willing to come out and give the presentations, even after the murder," Kate said.

I nodded.

"I wondered about that. I thought for sure you'd bow out after Francie died." She pulled a pair of gloves out of her pocket and put them on. "So, what's the problem?"

I shifted my weight and glanced out at the apple trees.

Beside me, Doug cleared his throat.

I'd better get this over with. "It's, well, it's been suggested that it's suspicious that you not only planned this time for your friends to be together at the orchard but also found Francie's body." My words tumbled out too fast, but at least I'd said it.

Kate's eyes widened. "And that I might be the killer?" Her voice rose in disbelief, and Bella's ears perked up.

"Libby was hesitant to even mention it," Doug said quickly. "We wanted to give you a chance to respond and get your thoughts on what may have actually happened."

Kate rested a hand on my arm. "Trust me, Libby. I'm not the killer. I want whoever it is caught as much as you do. Maybe more. I feel very guilty about the whole situation. The group would never have been together, and Francie may have never been killed if I hadn't set up this extra time for us at the reunion."

"We can't know that," I said, although she did have a point.

"You're very kind." Kate gave a soft smile, but she still sounded like she felt guilty. "And I do see, based on how it looks from the outside, that I look suspicious, but I don't even remember coming up with the idea for extending the reunion."

That seemed odd. "You don't?"

"No, I was talking with one of my friends one day, and then all of a sudden I was arranging things."

"You know," Doug said, "sometimes, either intentionally or unintentionally, someone can plant a seed in our mind without us even knowing it. We come away thinking something was our idea when really it wasn't."

Kate's eyes narrowed. "Yes, I've used that technique with a customer or two, especially when I think they may be looking at houses they can't afford. Just a really subtle suggestion. I let them connect the dots and ... gosh, you know, that may have been what happened."

I looked over at Doug, impressed. That sounded exactly like what someone might do if they were planning a murder. It made the killer seem completely innocent, and it got someone else to arrange to have the victim and other suspects all in one place. "Who were you talking with that day?"

"I feel bad telling you. Their comment may have been made in total innocence—just someone wanting to see old friends."

"But it might not have been," Doug said. "It might have been the first step in a plan to kill Francie."

Kate twisted her hands together. After a few moments, she let out a soft groan. "Tabitha." She quickly went on. "But I really don't think she's the killer. I mean, she did always compete with Francie in school, but she's got a big heart and I've known her for years and ..." Her voice trailed off as if she'd had the same thought I had, that if the killer wasn't some mysterious trespasser, it had to be someone she'd known for years.

An awkward position to be in. "When was this?"

Kate gazed off to one side. "It must have been late April. I know I made arrangements to rent the retreat center at the beginning of May."

"Thank you for telling me," I said. "And thanks for being so understanding about my questions. I do appreciate your point about Tabitha being kind-hearted, but I'd still like to ask her some more questions."

"Maybe that would be for the best," Kate said slowly. "If you'll be careful. I mean, I don't think she killed Francie, but if she did and she thinks you suspect her ..."

"I'll be careful," I assured her.

"She and Chad and Jessica were going to the local discount store this morning. I'm not sure what they were shopping for, but they each wanted to go."

"Tomorrow's Saturday. Maybe I'll come out then," I said.

"Well, be sure you come out early. Both deputies are coming with us, but we're watching the Homecoming parade tomorrow morning, going to a tailgate party for lunch, and then attending the ball game. They're honoring Chad. He was unsure about attending, but we convinced him that Francie would want him to be there."

"Good to know," I said. "And please, can you keep my sleuthing a secret?"

"No problem. I hope you figure this out." She zipped her coat up all the way. "I'm heading back inside. That wind is freezing." She patted Bella's head and hurried toward the retreat center.

Doug, Bella, and I walked toward the parking area.

"You know," I said, "Tabitha's claim that she didn't know Francie had sabotaged her chance at a job at Channel 7 could have been a lie."

"And having someone you considered an old friend keep you from getting a job you really wanted, especially in a business as competitive as broadcast journalism, could make a very strong motive for murder," Doug added.

The more I thought about it, the more it made sense. "So, Tabitha could have orchestrated the whole reunion to give her an opportunity for revenge." I opened the door for Bella to climb into my car, then turned to Doug. "But I think, instead of talking to Tabitha, I want to talk to Chad."

"Chad?"

"I want to ask him how long ago Tabitha tried for the job at Channel 7."

"Oh, I like where you're going with that," Doug said.

"Yeah. If Tabitha applied for the job a couple of months ago, say in July, there's no way that she hinted to Kate about a reunion way back in the spring in order to set up a time to kill Francie."

Doug nodded. "But if she applied for the job earlier, say in March, and then learned that Francie sabotaged her chances, she could have subtly gotten Kate to think about getting their old history club together on purpose."

"She might have intentionally planted the idea of the reunion in order to have the opportunity to kill Francie."

"Good thinking, Libby. Very logical."

"Thanks." I grinned at him.

"I wish we could talk to Chad now." Doug glanced at his watch. "But I've got a meeting."

"That's okay. I can't either." I had to drop off Bella with Sam and get to the museum. "I'll see if Sam can come with me tomorrow morning and the two of us can talk to Chad."

"Sounds good," Doug said.

I waved goodbye and drove Bella over to Sam's house, where I unloaded her water bowl, her favorite stuffed chicken, and a small plastic container I'd used to pack a few treats.

Sam must have been watching for me because he opened the door while I was still walking up the steps of the pale peach Victorian. The house, called Ashlington, was one I knew well. It had been built by my ancestors, and my aunt had sold it to Sam before I'd moved to town.

Bella let out a happy bark and bolted toward him, rolling on her back to get her tummy rubbed.

He seemed equally happy to have her visit, and when I returned at the end of the workday to pick her up, he apologized for the fact that we couldn't do something in the evening. With lots of alums in town, his department was hosting an event that he had to attend.

"I'd invite you, but"—he rolled his eyes—"I know who's running it. It's going to be long and dull."

I chuckled, grateful to skip it, and he readily agreed to pick me up at eight-thirty the next morning so we could go to the orchard to talk with Chad.

When I got home, the leak in my faucet was fixed, and the repairman had left a note saying he'd noticed the dog bowls and thanking me for keeping my pet out of the apartment for the day.

If only solving a murder was as easy as getting a leaky faucet repaired.

Tomorrow, though, hopefully, we could get some answers.

Chapter Ten

THE NEXT MORNING, Cleo surprised me by popping downstairs bright and early in running shoes, telling me she was starting a new exercise plan, and volunteering to take Bella out for a walk. I must have seemed stressed because even when I suggested the three of us go together, Cleo waved the idea aside and told me to use the time to relax. I gratefully accepted. I took a hot shower and made a big grocery list, including essentials like shortbread cookies and frozen enchiladas.

True to his word, Sam arrived at eight thirty to take Bella and me to the orchard. He might have looked a little sleepy when I opened the door to my apartment, but he was right on time.

"Up late last night?" I asked.

"You know me, I love to stay up and tinker with ideas. And late at night when it's quiet, I lose all track of time. If you ever doubt how much I love you, remember my willingness to go sleuthing early on a Saturday when I could sleep in."

I hugged him, and Bella circled him, nuzzling his legs with her head to let him know how much she, too, appreciated his sacrifice.

His mouth twisted to one side. "I've got bad news, though, about the yellow house where Doris's mother lived."

I glanced at my phone. "We'd better head out if we want to talk to Chad before the alums go to the ball game. Why don't you tell me on the way?"

Outside, the morning was gray and cool, almost cold. We hurried to his car, and Sam opened the door for Bella to climb into the back seat. Her plaid stadium blanket was spread out on the leather seats, all ready for her.

Once we were driving, he glanced over at me. "I looked up the owner of the yellow house online and tried calling last night but didn't get a reply. Then I realized that a colleague who works in civil engineering lives on that same street. I emailed him, and there was a message waiting for me when I got up this morning."

"And?"

"That house had been owned by an elderly couple. The husband passed away last spring, and the wife just died. Now the property is part of a complicated legal dispute. My friend gave me the name of one of the heirs, but apparently, there are two sons fighting over the house, and they disagree on everything. If one agrees to let us in, the other is bound to say no. So, until one of them is the official owner of the house, we may be stuck."

"You mean we found the right house, but that's all? We can't find the brick in the fireplace and look behind it for the diary?"

"That's what it sounds like."

My shoulders slumped. "More waiting. How frustrating."

Sam slowed as he passed a mom walking on the sidewalk holding the hands of two small children. I gazed over at him, struck anew with what a good guy he was to be so careful.

"I'll contact the heir I've got the name and number for. Who knows? Maybe the legal dispute will be resolved faster than they think."

"I guess you're right." I blew out a long exhale. "Hold on." I sent a quick text to Ester to let her know not to expect immediate progress. "And I guess we've got another mystery to focus on at the moment."

"We do indeed," Sam said.

Before long, we turned into the orchard.

"Wait," I said. "Don't drive to the retreat center. Chad, Kate, and Noah are over there by the farm market."

Sam backed up slightly and turned into the gravel parking area for the market.

"I've been meaning to get out here to buy some apples after you told me they were so good. At least that gives us a reason for stopping by."

"Excellent."

Sam opened the back passenger-side door for Bella, and the three of us walked over toward the market. The sky looked like a flat gray blanket, and a cold wind had picked up.

Noah, Kate, and Chad stood close together, talking. Kate wasn't wearing any makeup, which was odd. I'd never seen her without it. And Chad's mouth was drawn up tight.

An odd tingling ran down the back of my neck. "Are you all still going to the parade later?"

Chad shook his head.

Bella moved toward him and looked up expectantly.

He petted her head but seemed distracted.

"We hadn't even thought of the parade yet. We're all looking for Tabitha," Kate said.

Sam stepped closer. "Tabitha's missing?"

"Her car is still here." Noah pointed toward the retreat center. "But nobody's seen her since last night. The deputies split us into three groups, and we started searching about ten minutes ago."

My chest tightened, and I glanced over at Sam.

He nodded.

"We'll help," I offered. "Where should we look?"

"We'll go across the driveway, through those rows of trees over there." Noah pointed. "You two take the area here around the market. I don't know why she would have gone inside, but all you need to do to get into the market is push the code in the door. It's 1-2-3-4."

"Mmmm." Sam's shoulders stiffened.

From what he'd told me, no one hated lax security like

someone who'd worked in tech. A code of 1-2-3-4 was unacceptable.

"I'll text you if we find her," I told Noah.

In the distance, I heard Jessica shouting Tabitha's name.

Noah, Chad, and Kate walked west and also began yelling for Tabitha, and Bella sniffed at the ground, then pulled me toward the farm market.

"Should we …?" I looked at Sam and pointed to Bella.

"Sure," Sam said. "See where she goes."

"Okay." I walked along behind Bella, but I also started calling out Tabitha's name.

We drew a few feet closer to the farm market, and Bella began barking.

Then she lunged toward the door and began scratching at the base of it.

My heart rate sped.

"Hold on, Bella." Sam punched the code into the door lock.

As soon as the door was open, Bella darted in, dragging me along. She passed a stack of apple baskets, some broken wooden crates, and a bin of paper sacks, then stopped at a large metal door, where she looked up at me and whined.

"What's that?" It looked like a commercial refrigerator.

"I imagine it's a cold storage area for the apples." Sam opened the door. Cool air rushed out, along with the sweet smell of apples.

Bella lay down outside the door, head on her front paws, and whined even louder.

My stomach tightened, and Sam and I stepped inside.

There, about six feet from the door, lay Tabitha. She was sprawled on the floor, a gash sliced into her temple, and a pool of blood surrounded her head.

"Oh no!" I rushed forward and felt her neck.

There was no pulse.

And her skin was icy.

Chapter Eleven

MY HANDS SHOOK as we backed out of the cold storage area. When I tried to call Kate, my phone didn't even recognize my fingers as human. Finally, after warming them against my neck, I was able to dial.

"We found her," I said to Kate. "In the farm market. But it's—it's too late. Can you let everyone know?"

Kate let out a cry, then said she would.

I hung up.

Sam slid an arm around my waist, led me over to a worn, wooden chair, and eased me into a sitting position. "You look wobbly. You'd better sit for a while." He patted his hand against his thigh. "Bella, come over here by Libby."

Bella walked slowly to my side with her head lowered. She rested her chin on my leg, nestled her body close to me, and gazed up at me.

I patted her and let out a long, slow breath. The situation might be horrible, but at least I had Sam and Bella with me.

One of the sheriff's team, a dark-haired guy in his forties who introduced himself as Deputy Lewis, was the first to arrive, followed by Noah.

Lewis was probably the deputy who took the night patrol at the orchard.

His eyes narrowed, but he seemed calm as he assessed the situation. He called for an ambulance and the sheriff and then sent Sam, Bella, and me to the retreat center with Deputy Miller.

"The sheriff says for you all to sit in here." Deputy Miller gestured toward the living room.

I winced. The old farmhouse smelled like homemade bread—bread that surely Tabitha had made. Numbly, I walked toward a blue-patterned sofa and sank into it. Sam sat beside me, and Bella settled in front of us just as Chad and Kate arrived.

Chad's face was gray, his eyes sunken. "Tabitha too?" he asked in a husky voice.

"Yeah," I said, wishing there was an easier way to break the news.

Kate grabbed a green afghan off the other couch. "I know it doesn't make sense, but I feel like I should take this to Tabitha to help her get warm."

Deputy Miller's eyes widened. "The EMTs will be with her, ma'am. They'll take care of, um, anything she needs. Why don't you sit down?"

Kate clutched the afghan against her chest and sat next

to me on the couch.

Bella rubbed her head against Kate's leg. Kate petted her but seemed like she was on autopilot, not really there.

I patted her arm. "I'm so sorry, Kate."

"I kept telling myself that maybe Tabitha had gone out for a walk and twisted her ankle or something." She stroked the afghan. "I can't believe she's dead too."

A few seconds later Derek and Jessica arrived. Jessica was pale, her hands shaking. Derek seemed to have gone back to his calm-in-a-crisis mode.

"Deputy Lewis asked one of us to watch for the ambulance," Derek said. "Hannah went to do that, and he told Jessica and me to come here."

"Did he say anything else?" Sam asked.

"No," Derek said. "But Noah said that if Tabitha was unconscious and couldn't leave the chiller, she would have suffocated. Something about how there's less oxygen in there to make the apples last longer."

Deputy Miller cleared his throat. "You all need to sit quietly and wait until the sheriff arrives. He'll want to talk to each of you about the vic—about Tabitha."

Jessica let out a sob and dashed toward the other couch, where she curled up in a ball, face hidden.

The deputy paused awkwardly and ran a hand over his mouth as if he wished he'd spoken more carefully.

Derek sat down beside Jessica and put his hand on her shoulder, his jaw tight.

I looked from one alum to the other.

I'd really thought Tabitha was the killer. Thought she'd

been angry about the position at Channel 7. Thought she'd subtly gotten Kate to set up the reunion so she could exact her revenge.

Instead, Tabitha had been exactly what she appeared to be—a nice TV anchor who liked to bake.

Everything I'd thought had been wrong. And now Tabitha was dead.

I sank back into the couch cushions and closed my eyes.

A few minutes later, the sheriff's cowboy boots made sharp, almost metallic clicks as he stepped into the tiled hall, then more muffled taps as he walked onto the hardwood floor of the living room. His lips were tight, and his eyes moved from one person to the next.

"Miss Ballard," he said in a hard voice, "didn't I make myself clear about interfering in my investigations?"

Bella rose to her feet, her muscles taut, and Sam wrapped an arm around my shoulders. "Libby came with me," he said. "I wanted to buy apples."

The sheriff's eyes narrowed, and he crossed his arms over his chest. "Right." Sarcasm dripped from his voice. "You two being here is just a coincidence."

"That's correct," Sam said.

"And it's a good thing we were here," I added. "We offered to help, and Bella led us to the body."

"Bella?" Billy Harper's voice softened, and his eyes widened. He glanced at the deputy, who nodded.

Billy pointed at Sam and me. "Let's go in the dining room."

We followed him across the hall, and Bella padded along behind us.

The sheriff sat on one side of the dining room table, and Sam and I took spots across from him.

"Start at the beginning. Tell me exactly what happened after you arrived here." He opened a notepad and pulled out a pen. The swagger of our first meeting had faded. Realizing that your failure to catch a killer had allowed a second murder to occur could do that to a person.

Sam looked over at me, and I began, starting with how we'd noticed Chad, Kate, and Noah near the farm market when we'd first driven in. With as many details as I could recall, I explained the rest of what had happened.

The sheriff scribbled one more note, then set down his pen and looked at Sam. "Is that accurate? The way you would describe it?"

"Yep," Sam said.

"Nothing to add?" the sheriff asked.

"Nothing."

The sheriff's face tightened, and he looked at me. "I do see why Uncle John respects you. I hardly ever get a witness who notices so many details." He looked over at Bella and shook his head, then spoke more loudly. "And this dog ..."

Bella stood, and I patted her back.

"From now on, no more of those history talks you've been coming out to give in the mornings."

"But I have more prepared."

"Absolutely not." He scolded me with a pointed finger.

"For your own safety, you need to stay away from this place."

I opened my mouth to say more but stopped. Maybe he was right.

Billy walked over to Bella and scratched behind her ears. "Good dog," he murmured to her. Then he gestured for Sam and me to stand. "You're free to go home now. And I suggest you do just that."

Sam grabbed our jackets from the living room, and we headed toward his car.

We passed Deputy Lewis, who was standing near the picnic area, talking on his phone.

He lowered his voice, but I could still make out what he said. "... he's ignoring evidence that doesn't fit his narrative, no matter what we tell him. He's refusing help from his uncles and state investigators. He doesn't have a clue who the killer is, and he's—" He glanced up and saw me. "Call you later," he said into his phone. He shoved it in his pocket and scowled at me.

Sam and I got Bella settled in the back seat, then climbed into his car.

As soon as we were out on Orchard Road, I turned to him. "Did you hear what the deputy said?"

"I did." He shook his head. "Billy Harper is all hung up in his own ego. A colleague of mine told me that his dad, the former sheriff, was really well respected. It seems Billy's so busy trying to live up to his father that he's not listening to what his own team tells him. And he's nowhere near solving this case."

My shoulders slumped. "Neither are we."

Why had I ever believed I could solve this crime? I'd been way off base, suspecting the wrong person, and now there was a second victim, a second life cut short.

A wave of guilt washed through me, and I looked over at Sam. "I should have done something, should have figured out how to stop this."

"It's not your fault," he said.

I shook my head. Technically, he was right, but it didn't make the feeling go away. No matter what the sheriff said, no matter how shocked I felt, I had to keep trying. I had to figure this out. I had to stop the killer before someone else ended up dead.

Sam took Bella and me home, then headed out to Ashlington, where he said he'd be grading homework assignments all weekend.

I wandered around my apartment, reliving the discovery of Tabitha's body. Eventually, I realized I had to get my mind off the image of her lying there dead. I tried a crossword, even tried watching an old episode of *Antiques Road Show*. Nothing helped.

Finally, I sat down with Bella on my living room floor. I brushed her fur until it gleamed, trimming out some stubborn burrs that wouldn't comb out along the way.

She didn't like me dealing with those burrs, but once we were done, she licked my hand and gazed up at me with love.

She looked better, and I felt better. Time with my dog, who made me feel like the most important person on the planet, always eased my troubles. My mind was still on the murder, but I'd moved past the shock.

I put one of my favorite '70s albums on my dad's old turntable and settled into my regular Saturday routine of cleaning my apartment, all the while thinking about who would want to kill both Francie and Tabitha.

But I didn't have a clue.

I had just finished mopping my kitchen floor when my phone rang with a call from Hannah. "Libby?"

"Is there news? Did the sheriff make an arrest?"

"No." Her voice was tight. "He's taken Noah in for questioning."

"Noah?" I sank onto the couch.

I'd never even considered Noah as a suspect. "Why would Noah have killed Francie and Tabitha? He'd never even met them before they came for the reunion."

Hannah drew in an audible breath. "Apparently, he knew Francie."

My stomach tensed. "Noah knew Francie before she came to the orchard?"

"Back in St.—St. Louis," Hannah stammered. "And he kept it a secret."

Chapter Twelve

MY CHEST FELT HOLLOW. Secrets in a marriage were never a good thing, and the fact that Noah hadn't told Hannah he had a history with Francie was particularly bad, given the situation. "Tell me what happened."

"After the sheriff talked to everyone and they took Tabitha's body away," Hannah said, "Chad stopped by our house to tell us the internet was out at the retreat center. While he was there, I guess he noticed a photo that we have up in the living room. It's from when Noah and I were first married, back when he didn't have a beard. Chad didn't say anything, but he recognized Noah from that picture. He talked with Derek and then called the sheriff."

"But how did Noah know Francie?" I asked.

"He didn't actually know her personally. Chad recognized Noah from an exposé that Francie did five years ago. It was a story she was especially proud of, so she'd shown it to Chad several times. That exposé destroyed Noah's business."

Oh wow. I had not seen this coming. "And you had no idea?"

"No. I met Noah four years ago online. Before that, Noah had been the owner of a restaurant in St. Louis. It failed, and I always thought that was because it didn't have enough business. He never said much about it, simply that he'd learned from his mistakes and wanted to move on. He seemed embarrassed, so I didn't push."

Which was probably what I would have done. "No need to make someone dwell on a failure."

"That's what I thought. Noah and I hit it off so fast that we were married fifteen months after we met. He moved down from St. Louis and loved working with me at the orchard. He had great ideas, like developing the retreat center and adding a Christmas light display to provide new income streams."

"But what was the exposé?"

"I don't know the whole story, but something illegal went on at the restaurant, and Francie uncovered it in a big investigative journalism piece." Hannah gave a huge sigh. "Now I feel all confused. Part of me is horrified that they suspect the man I've loved for years. I can't fathom him as a killer. But part of me feels betrayed that he never told me he'd been involved in something criminal."

I sat back on the couch. It did sound like Noah had a motive for killing Francie. If Tabitha had figured out that he was the killer, he'd have had a motive for killing her too.

"Hold on. You and Noah went to get the food for dinner together. How could he have killed Francie if he was with you?"

"We weren't together the whole time," Hannah said in a low voice. "I had to go to the big kitchen pantry at the retreat center to get napkins. It took longer than I expected because they were on a high shelf, and I had to climb on a chair to reach them."

"Oh." So, Noah didn't have an alibi for Francie's death.

"To be honest, I guess theoretically he could have slipped out last night after I went to sleep and killed Tabitha. Running the orchard is so much physical labor that I sleep really soundly every night." She hesitated. "Although I doubt I'll sleep at all tonight."

So, a motive and no alibi for either murder. I could understand why the sheriff had brought Noah in for questioning.

"I've called Uncle Doug," Hannah said. "He says he'll get Noah a lawyer."

"That's good. And you need to talk to Noah and give him a chance to explain what the exposé was about."

"I'm sitting in the parking lot outside the sheriff's office. I went in, but they told me I couldn't see him."

"Surely they will eventually let you see him. Will you tell me what you learn? Or if there's a chance I can talk with him?"

"I will."

"Good," I said. "Try not to jump to conclusions. Things might not be as bad as you think." I hung up.

I'd done my best to sound convincing.

But honestly, if I were Hannah, I'd be afraid I'd married a murderer.

Overnight the temperature plummeted. When Cleo offered to take Bella for a walk before she went to church, claiming that having her along made the new exercise routine more bearable, I gladly agreed. I didn't even offer to join them.

Instead, I snuggled under a warm blanket on my couch while the wind whistled through the trees outside. I drank a mug of strong, dark tea and thought about Noah and Hannah. With my background, having been married to a man who lied to me and cheated on me, I really felt for Hannah. Trust was hard, especially when someone had been keeping secrets.

Thank goodness Sam didn't keep secrets. Well, except for the surprise he was planning, the donation to the museum. That was a different level of secret, more like a Christmas present.

Shortly before lunch, Hannah called to tell me that she'd been able to talk to Noah and that he'd been released. "He wants to explain what happened to you and Doug and Alice in person. Can you come out to the orchard about two?"

I sat up. "Sure."

"Bring Bella. She's such a sweetie."

I was just about to ask what Noah had said when she hung up.

Time crawled as I ate my lunch, but at one thirty, I grabbed a sweater, and Bella and I headed out to the orchard. We met Doug and Alice outside Noah and Hannah's farmhouse.

Hannah opened the front door as we walked up the steps. "Come in," she said. "Let's sit in the kitchen."

The smaller farmhouse had clearly been built recently, but it was furnished in the same cozy, country style as the historic retreat center. A fire burned in the living room fireplace, popping and crackling from time to time. We settled into chairs around a large oak table in the adjoining dining room with Noah on one end and Hannah at the other. Bella flopped down on the floor beside my chair.

"Thanks for coming out," Noah said. "I wanted to explain to you all what happened. And I have to apologize, Doug and Alice, for never telling you this before."

He looked somewhat worse for wear after being held overnight in the county jail. His eyes were bloodshot and had dark circles under them.

Alice patted his arm, but Doug gave only a tight nod. "You've put Hannah through quite a lot. I'm eager to hear what you have to say."

"Well," Noah's voice shook a little as he began. "Unlike what Hannah thought, my restaurant in Saint Louis was quite popular. We offered a relaxed atmosphere serving gourmet takes on classic American favorites. It was near a shopping mall and was usually packed at lunch and dinner. And we made a pork tenderloin sandwich that was even better than the one served at the Dogwood Café."

Hard to believe, but maybe to his palate it had been.

Noah glanced around. "This is kind of a long story. I'm sorry."

"Take your time, dear," Alice said. "We want to understand what happened."

"Thanks." He sat up a little taller. "So, the problem started because my manager hired a server named Julie Ann. She was around thirty, obviously experienced in the business. At first, she seemed great. She never messed up an order, was wonderful with customers, had people asking to sit at one of her tables. What we didn't know was that Julie Ann was a scammer. Two or three times a week, she'd get a credit card from a patron to run through the machine to pay a bill, and she'd secretly detour by the bathroom and take a photo of the front and back of the card with her phone."

Doug's eyebrows pinched together, and Hannah's jaw tightened as if the very thought of it made her angry.

"Julie Ann picked her victims by looking for someone who had a shopping bag. If the customer had a shopping bag from, say, the nearby big department store, she would later run a charge for one item at the online version of that department store on their card. She never used a card more than once. Because the charges were never huge and were from familiar stores, she got away with it for months. Some items she kept, some items she sold online."

"Very sneaky," I said.

Noah nodded. "I don't know how long this would have gone on except one day she ran the scam on Francie. From what Francie said in her exposé, she carefully checked her credit card bills every month. She got reimbursed for some of her clothes because she wore them on camera."

"That makes sense," Alice said.

Noah continued. "Julie Ann saw that Francie had a bag from a specialty chain called Classic Styles, and she assumed Francie had used her Visa there. But Francie always used the Classic Styles store credit card because even when the TV station reimbursed her for the dressier purchases, she earned points that she could use to buy clothes for casual wear."

"I know people who travel for my company who do that at hotels," Doug said. "They rack up enough points to get free stays for their own vacations. It's a small perk that hopefully makes up a bit for the time they spend away from their families."

I'd known people who did that too.

"Anyway, when Francie saw that her VISA was used at Classic Styles, she knew it wasn't right. When she checked, she knew she hadn't made a purchase that day. Based on the timing of when the credit card charge went through, she suspected her card number was stolen through the restaurant. Most people would have gone to the police, but Francie was an investigative journalist."

"So, she went undercover?" I scooted my chair closer.

"She thought she might be recognized, so she assembled a team to help her. One member took a job as a server at the restaurant, and three others went there to eat. Eventually, they figured out what was going on, realized the problem was Julie Ann, and took the information to the police. But they also ran a big exposé on the evening news."

"The bad publicity ruined Noah's restaurant," Hannah said.

Alice looked at Noah. "You didn't actually do anything illegal?"

"No," Noah said, "but I felt horrible, especially for my staff who lost their jobs. Maybe if I had done a better job overseeing things, none of it would have happened." He grimaced. "I was mad for a long time—mad at Julie Ann, mad at Francie, and mad at myself. But eventually, I accepted what had happened, realized Francie was just doing her job, and I moved on with my life." He glanced down the table at Hannah. "And things got a lot better after I met you."

Hannah's eyes shone.

"You can imagine how shocked I was," he said, "when I saw Francie at the orchard and found out she and Hannah had been friends in college. At first, I thought she might recognize me as well. But time had gone by, I'd grown a beard, and I was in an orchard in south-central Missouri, not a restaurant in St. Louis. She never gave any indication that she knew who I was."

"Why didn't you tell Hannah about this a long time ago?" Doug asked.

Noah dipped his head, then looked back up. "I was embarrassed. I wanted her to think well of me and ... I'd been really stupid."

"You were a victim just as much as the people who got scammed," Alice said.

"That's a kind way to think of it, but it was bad management." He gave a rueful smile. "When the alumni arrived at the orchard, it seemed like a poor time to bring it up. I was afraid Hannah would feel awful for agreeing to host them since it was a reminder of such a dreadful time in my past."

"I would have felt terrible," Hannah said. "I never would have agreed to have all of them here if I'd known what Francie had done to you." She let out a heavy sigh. "Anyone else would have gone to the police. They would have handled it more quietly, and maybe your restaurant would have survived."

"Maybe," Noah said. "The only good thing that came out of it was that once I was no longer running the restaurant, I had time to look online for someone to date. If Francie hadn't done her exposé, I never would have met you."

Noah and Hannah exchanged a long, warm glance. However betrayed she may have felt earlier, she had clearly forgiven him.

And I did believe good things could come out of a bad situation. A second chance could land you in a better place than where you started. Look at me, moving to Dogwood Springs.

Still, Noah was in an awkward spot. "So, the sheriff suspects you because you have a motive."

"Yeah," Noah said. "And no solid alibi for the time of either murder."

"They came out this morning with a warrant and

searched our house and the barn," Hannah said. "They took a lot of papers, stuff I'd never even seen before. I guess it had to do with Noah's old business. I ... I couldn't stop them."

She shot Noah a look of apology.

Doug sat back in his chair. "Thanks for explaining, Noah. I'm sorry you went through all that and lost your restaurant."

"Thanks." Noah gave a wry smile. "All I can do now is try to move forward and help Hannah make a success of the orchard."

"Which isn't going to be easy with two murders committed here within the past week." Hannah crossed her arms over her stomach as if she felt ill just thinking about their financial situation.

"Plus, I hate to say it," I added, "but if the sheriff is trying to prove that Noah is the murderer, he may not be looking at any other suspects. He may be no closer to finding the real killer." I paused. "And neither are we."

Alice's eyes tensed. "You're not giving up, are you, Libby?"

Hannah and Noah looked even more stressed.

"No, I'm not." I was too stubborn, and this mattered too much. It was about justice, about truth. "But I'm not sure what direction to go next. I guess I have to think."

"We'll all think," Doug said.

"I'll text the rest of our group and explain what Noah told us." Alice held up her phone. "I bet someone will come up with an idea."

I agreed, rather half-heartedly, and walked to the car with Bella.

As I was pulling into my driveway, my phone dinged with a text.

Zeke Anderson
We need to go to the café. Marcus knows something. Just gotta get him to spill.

My pulse quickened.

A flurry of texts followed as we arranged to meet at the Dogwood Café for dinner so we could talk to the owner.

We had a new lead in our investigation.

Chapter Thirteen

SHORTLY BEFORE IT was time to meet at the café, Cleo came downstairs to walk there with me. Before we left, I gave Bella her dinner, let her out briefly, and explained to her that she had to stay home. It was far too cold to sit outside on the patio, and the café didn't allow dogs inside.

Which didn't make Bella happy.

She snuggled up with her favorite comfort toy, a stuffed chicken, and shot me one of those how-can-you-possibly-leave-me looks.

I rubbed her ears and promised her I'd be home soon.

The minute Cleo and I entered the café, the contrast between the cozy space and the cold outside was striking. Outside, it was in the low forties with a howling wind. Inside, the room was mostly full and every so often, the buzz of the espresso machine interrupted the quiet hum of conversation. The cocoa-brown walls, the gleaming wooden tables, and the aroma of the day's special of vegetable beef soup combined to make me feel like I was being wrapped in a hug.

"It looks like Alice and Doug already have our favorite indoor table." Cleo pointed to the corner farthest from the door.

"Great!" I led the way over. Alice and Doug sat across from each other at one end of the table. Cleo and I took the middle seats. Before I even had my coat hanging on the back of my chair, Sam and Zeke joined us, with Zeke sliding in beside Cleo and Sam sitting by me.

"Hey, Sam." Cleo leaned forward. "Did you get your HVAC problem solved?"

"I did." He let out a long sigh. "Everything's good."

Cleo beamed, and although Zeke was studying the menu, Doug and Alice also looked happy.

I glanced over at him. "HVAC?"

"Uh, nothing major, except the bill since it was an emergency visit on the weekend." He rubbed the back of his neck. "I called Cleo to get a recommendation of a reliable local service."

"I didn't know who to suggest," Cleo said. "But Bryce recently had a problem at his veterinary clinic and came up with a name. I double-checked with Alice, and it sounds like we were able to help Sam deal with the crisis."

Poor guy, having to deal with no heat on top of all the grading he'd mentioned. I reached over and squeezed his hand.

A moment later, a server appeared, and we ordered drinks and dinner. Then I looked up and down the table.

"Thanks so much for meeting with me. I wanted us to regroup to try to figure this out."

"I appreciate it," Doug said. "Even though the lawyer kept the sheriff from arresting Noah, Hannah is worried sick."

Sam looked across the table at Zeke. "Why do you think Marcus might be able to help us?"

"I was talking with my girlfriend, Zoe, last night," Zeke said. "I told her that if we rule out Hannah and Noah, we only have three suspects left—Chad, Kate, and the trespasser."

"Wait." Doug held up a finger. "Did we completely eliminate Jessica and Derek?"

Good question. "If we include them, they would have had to have worked together since they each provided an alibi for the other for Francie's murder."

"That seems unlikely," Sam said. "They both would need a motive or one of them would need a motive strong enough to convince the other to lie. I can't picture Derek helping Jessica kill Francie simply because Francie was mean to her twenty-five years ago."

"I can't either," Alice said.

"Zoe had a great idea," Zeke continued. "She thought that the alums probably went out to eat and that a server might have overheard something that would be a clue."

"Very smart." I loved the fact that Zeke was giving Zoe full credit. Not every teenage boy—or grown man—would have done that.

"Zoe said that the Pit & Pickle and the Dogwood Café

were the most popular restaurants in town, but that the Pit & Pickle is really loud. She thought we should look at the café."

Everyone nodded.

"She called her friend Celia, who works here part-time after school. Celia remembered that one evening Marcus made a big deal about waiting on a former Grove University quarterback who came in for dinner, a quarterback who had an undefeated season. I looked it up online, and that had to be Chad."

Sam gave a wry smile. "That 11-0 season twenty-five years ago was the only undefeated season Grove University ever had, sadly just about the only good season."

"The online site basically said the same thing," Zeke said. "So, Zoe and I ran over here and ordered dessert. I asked Marcus if he'd overheard anything when Chad was here." Zeke shook his head. "He denied it, but I think I asked him wrong. He knows something. I'm sure of it."

"No need to beat yourself up," Doug said. "We can try again."

Our server walked up to the table with our drinks, and Sam asked if Marcus was available.

"He's in the kitchen dealing with a late delivery from a supplier. I'll tell him that you'd like him to stop by."

We thanked her, and she told us our meals would be out shortly.

I wrapped my hands around my tea mug to warm them while it steeped.

"While we wait, I can add some information that I found last night online," Sam said.

"Oh, what did you learn?" Alice asked.

"I'd say renting out the retreat center for her friends was no hardship for Kate," Sam said. "Even if the real estate market goes down, I'd expect her company does well. In addition to sales, it also does a lot of property management. And it's quite substantial, with branches all over the Kansas City area."

That fit with my impression of Kate as well.

"I also found Derek online," Sam added. "He's well-known in the area of academic integrity. Even though he's a dean, he still does research about plagiarism, especially related to artificial intelligence, and he presents at a lot of conferences."

"You know"—Alice leaned in—"to me, that's an even stronger reason to rule him out as a suspect. I can't see someone who's devoted his life's work to professional ethics as the killer."

"That makes sense," Cleo said.

Our server returned with our food. Cleo, Doug, Zeke, and I had all ordered the day's special, a bowl of vegetable beef soup and half a grilled cheese sandwich on sourdough bread. Alice had gotten a Cobb salad, and Sam had chosen a bacon cheeseburger and fries.

We quickly dug in. My sandwich was a golden masterpiece of gooey goodness, and the soup was truly exceptional —really good beef, a rich, flavorful broth, big chunks of potatoes and carrots, along with onions, green beans, corn, and peas. Both the soup and sandwich were absolutely delicious—comfort food at the highest level.

I'd just taken a big bite of my sandwich when Marcus walked up to our table. I chewed quickly and wiped my mouth.

A short, round, mostly bald man, he'd run the café for decades. He always remembered my name when I came in, but I didn't know him well.

Alice and Doug, though, greeted him like a dear friend.

"I heard you all had a question for me." Marcus looked up and down the table expectantly.

"It's kind of delicate." Doug stood. "If you have a moment, I'll grab you a chair so you can join us."

"Certainly." Marcus waved Doug back to his seat, pulled over a chair, and sat at the end of the table between him and Alice.

"You know how Hannah, who runs the Witley Historic Orchard with her husband, is my niece?" Doug asked.

"Sure do," Marcus said. "I get apples from her and Noah to use in our baking."

"Well, she's really upset about what's been going on at the orchard. I don't know if you've heard, but there was a second murder there yesterday."

"Yeah." Marcus glanced down. "We generally hear all the news first here at the café."

"That's why we wanted to talk to you." Alice took a quick sip of her coffee. "Libby's done such a great job in the past solving mysteries here in Dogwood Springs that Doug and I suggested Hannah ask for her help."

Marcus nodded.

"We heard that some of the alums, including Chad Weaver, the quarterback who led Grove University to an undefeated season twenty-five years ago, were in here the other day," I said. "I know you'd never intentionally eavesdrop, but I'm sure you accidentally overhear things. We wondered if there was any chance that you might have heard something that would help us."

Marcus shot a look at Zeke. Then he edged back in his chair, and his eyes grew wary.

"I know it may seem wrong to talk about your customers," Alice said, "but two people have died. This killer needs to be stopped."

"I did overhear something sensitive. It didn't make me think someone was the murderer, or I would have called the sheriff. But I can tell you what was said."

The rest of us leaned in.

"Chad Weaver was in here a couple of days ago, I think it was Friday, having lunch with a woman who I assume was one of the other alums. They looked to be about the same age, and she wasn't anyone local."

"What did she look like?" Cleo asked.

"Brown hair, about this long." He held a hand up to his chin. "All rounded over—"

"Like a mushroom?" I asked.

Marcus's eyes lit. "Exactly like that."

"That's Jessica," I said. "And yes, she is one of the alums staying at the orchard retreat center."

"She and Chad were talking about their spouses. The

woman—Jessica—was upset with her husband and wanted a divorce. Chad knew her husband or knew something about him. He said something like 'Now that I know the whole story, I've got my own reasons to dislike him, but I still think you should try to save your marriage. Go to counseling or something.'"

Zeke's face scrunched up. "His own reasons for disliking her husband … what does that mean?"

"I assumed he was bothered by how Jessica's husband was treating her," Marcus said.

"Did Chad say anything else?" Alice asked.

"It sounded like his marriage was rather awful. Francie Weaver always seemed so nice on TV, but apparently, she'd denigrated him for years, saying his glory days were behind him."

Doug winced, and he and Sam exchanged pained glances.

"Even so," Marcus continued, "Chad said that in spite of all that, in spite of the fact that Francie wanted to divorce him, he'd begged her to give their marriage another shot. I got the impression that he really loved her and believed that a couple could go through a rough patch and, if they worked at it, repair their relationship."

"Interesting," I said. "Did you hear anything else?"

"No. Lots of talk about how shocked they were that Francie was dead." He stood. "That's all I heard. I sure hope you can figure this out, but I do want you to know that I don't make a practice of gossiping about my customers."

Alice assured him that we knew he didn't, and he walked back toward the kitchen.

"So, Chad wasn't entirely honest about his relationship with Francie, was he?" Cleo said.

"No, he wasn't," I agreed. "He admitted they were having problems, but he definitely gave the impression that they'd work through things. Instead, it sounds like Francie wanted a divorce."

"That would have made all the cruel comments he'd endured even worse, wouldn't it?" Alice said.

"It would. But ..." I sat my spoon down in my soup bowl. "It also sounded like he hadn't given up hope on their relationship. That may have been an act, but Bella likes Chad, and it seems like she has some sort of sense about who's a good person."

Cleo scrunched up her face. "Bella is really smart, but she's also got a big heart. Maybe Chad is the killer, but he feels guilty, and Bella senses his pain."

Hmmm. Cleo could be right. "I know I'm not doing any more presentations at the orchard, but I'd sure like to talk to Chad."

"You could try a different approach and simply take all this to the sheriff," Sam suggested.

"I don't know if it would be enough to make Billy suspect Chad instead of Noah," Doug said.

"If I talk to Chad and learn he was alone in the orchard when Francie was killed, that will mean he had no alibi," I said. "That would make the case against him even stronger. I heard the sheriff interview him after Francie died, and he didn't ask that. And I can ask it in reverse as if I'm trying to make him look less guilty. Or as if I'm trying to see if one of the other alumni has an alibi."

Sam tipped his head to one side, then nodded as if I'd eased his worries.

"The salon is closed on Mondays," Cleo said. "I can go out there with you tomorrow."

"Thanks," I said. "That seems like a good plan." Cleo had taken those self-defense classes, and I'd have my pepper spray in my purse.

We were circling back to Chad, but this time, we knew he had a motive for murdering his wife.

And this time, hopefully, I could see through his lies.

We needed to get to the bottom of this mystery.

Chapter Fourteen

MONDAY MORNING, Cleo, Bella, and I returned to the orchard to talk to Chad.

I drove past the farm market, spotted him chatting with Jessica near the barn, and parked by the retreat center. The sky was overcast, but luckily the temperature had warmed up and the bitter wind of the previous evening was gone. Cleo, Bella, and I got out of my car and walked toward them.

At that moment, Chad's phone rang, blaring out the Grove University fight song. He glanced at the screen, muttered to Jessica, and strode away.

Jessica turned to us.

"We were hoping to talk to ..." Cleo waved a hand toward Chad's back.

"I think he'll be on the phone for a while," Jessica said. "That's the insurance company. There's quite a list of things he has to do to collect on Francie's life insurance, and he had questions about some of them."

I nodded. "That would be important."

"Yeah. Francie earned a lot more than Chad, and they bought a huge new house two years ago. He thinks the insurance will let him pay it off and give him some additional money to pour into his business," Jessica said. "Of course, it's not what he wanted, but at least some good can come from Francie's death."

My heart sped. Insurance money! I hadn't even thought of that as a reason Chad might have killed Francie. Depending on the size of that policy, it could be a huge motive. I was even more interested in talking to him.

After another minute, he walked back toward us, sliding his phone into his pocket.

Jessica headed back to the retreat center, and Chad started to go with her.

"Hey, Chad, wait." Cleo jogged a few steps toward him.

He turned.

I hurried over to them. "I, uh, I had to come back out today to bring something to Hannah," I lied.

"I came along to help carry it inside," Cleo added quickly.

Good save. "While I was here," I said, "I wanted to ask you something."

"Fire away." He bent down to pat Bella, then straightened and slid his hands into his back pockets.

Bella stared at him intently. Was she sensing he was the killer?

"I keep thinking about what's happened with Francie and Tabitha," I said. "I can't help but wonder if there's some clue the sheriff is missing. When Francie was killed, were you with anyone in the orchard? If you were, the sheriff could rule them out as a suspect."

"That's smart," Chad said. "I wish I could help, but I was alone most of the time, except for a brief chat with Tabitha about football."

"Oh, I see." I tried to sound disappointed, but I'd gotten exactly the information I needed, and—thanks to Jessica—even more. Chad had a strong motive to kill his wife because she was divorcing him even after he'd endured her abuse. He had an additional motive of her life insurance. And he had no alibi for the time of her murder. Surely the sheriff would listen to me when I told him why Chad was the killer.

Chad looked to one side, then back at me. "I can't believe how much I miss Francie. She was like a drug that I couldn't quit, even when she hurt me, even when she hurt other people. Like poor Jessica." He glanced toward the house.

"Jessica? Oh, you mean how Francie was cruel to her in college," I said. "Someone told me about that."

His brow furrowed. "No, I mean Francie went out of her way when we got here to 'accidentally' let it slip to Jessica that she was having an affair with her husband. It started after the four of us talked at an alumni event in St. Louis nine months ago."

My eyes nearly bugged out. "You're telling me that the

person Francie was having an affair with was Jessica's husband?"

"Yeah," Chad said. "Jessica didn't even know the affair was going on until she came here for the reunion. Heck, I had a pretty good idea Francie was seeing someone else, but I didn't know who it was until Jessica told me when we went out to lunch on Friday."

Wow. Francie had been cheating on Chad. And the conversation Marcus overheard—when Chad told Jessica he had his own reasons for disliking her husband—he'd meant the affair with Francie. "I'm so sorry."

"After Francie's comment, Jessica was furious. She called her husband and said she was having the worst school year of her life and that he should have been supporting her and instead he betrayed her. She told him she wanted a divorce."

I exchanged glances with Cleo, then looked back at Chad, who didn't seem to realize the importance of what he'd told us. "That's quite a motive for Jessica to commit murder. You might have been angry with Francie, and maybe you didn't know who she was having an affair with, but it sounds like you knew it had been going on for a while, right?"

"Yeah, but—"

"Jessica learned when she got to the reunion, just hours before the murder took place," I said.

Cleo nodded. "She would have been reeling, probably ready to kill her husband and Francie."

"Jessica didn't do it," Chad said.

My brilliant theory deflated as I realized he was right. "She had an alibi, didn't she? She was in the orchard with Derek. Wait ... Maybe he lied to protect her. Do you think he would?"

Chad blinked at me. "No. Never, but ..." He ran a hand over his chin.

"What? You think he actually would lie for her?"

"Not outright lie. But Derek did always have a soft spot for Jessica. He told me once that she reminded him of his little sister. I think he could have been fooled by her or given her the benefit of the doubt." He shook his head. "But that isn't what I meant. Jessica would never kill someone."

"Are you sure?" Cleo asked.

"I'm sure. She'd be too scared. Frankly, I was shocked she had the courage to say she wanted a divorce. It would have been more in character for her to keep enduring the infidelity. I thought about that a long time because it didn't make sense, and I finally decided that maybe this hadn't been the first time Jessica's husband had cheated on her."

"Or, maybe, Jessica developed a backbone as she got older," Cleo said. "Maybe she stood up for herself with her husband, and she also took revenge against Francie."

Chad shook his head. "No way. Nobody's personality changes that much after college."

I shoved my hands into my jacket pockets and thought for a moment. "I do tend to agree with you."

"I'll tell you what I told the sheriff. I really believe the killer was the trespasser, some crazy lovesick fan. And I guess Tabitha must have seen what happened." Chad held my gaze and spoke more slowly as if to make sure I understood. "Jessica wasn't the murderer." He gave Bella a quick pat on the head, spun on his heel, and strode toward the retreat center.

Cleo and I were quiet as we settled Bella in the back seat of my car and climbed in. When we were out on Orchard Road, I turned to Cleo. "That was quite a conversation."

"It sure was. Yesterday we had no real suspects, and now we have two."

"Two good ones," I said. "I still think Chad's the killer. Love turned to hate, plus greed for the insurance money. Those are strong motives. And he has no alibi."

"I don't know." Cleo ran a hand through her hair. "I think it's Jessica. Francie was horrid to her, practically slapping Jessica in the face with the fact that she was having an affair with her husband."

"But Jessica has an alibi." I tapped the steering wheel. "Well, a shaky alibi, I guess. It sounds like she could have fooled Derek into lying for her. So maybe we were wrong to rule out the two of them as suspects."

"Exactly. Anybody can be pushed too far, Libby. I think Jessica was. Chad just can't accept that someone he had been friends with when he was in college killed his wife. And Tabitha."

"Well, at the moment, I can't prove you wrong." I turned onto the highway toward town. "We've got to figure out which of them did it—and fast."

"We will." Cleo glanced at her phone, "But right now you probably need to get to work."

She was right.

I dropped her and Bella at home and then rushed to the museum.

Normally I had my life organized, but with all the turmoil after Tabitha had been killed, I'd forgotten to go to the grocery store over the weekend. At lunchtime, I drove home, let Bella out for a few minutes, and refilled her water bowl. Then I spent a few minutes telling her how much I loved her and scratching behind her ears the way she liked best.

I called in a carry-out order to the Dogwood Café, drove back to the museum, parked, and hurried down the street to pick it up, zipping up my coat and pulling on my gloves while I walked. The wind today felt icy.

On the way, I popped into the Dogwood Springs Bakery and bought a shortbread cookie. I'd recently learned they now had my favorites every day instead of only on Wednesdays. Then I headed to the café. Once I picked up my soup and sandwich combo, I could smell the carrot-ginger soup through the packaging. I walked even faster, eager for lunch but still able to appreciate how each downtown shop was decorated for fall.

I was admiring the display of spooky books, cuddly-looking stuffed-animal black cats, and friendly ghosts in the bookstore window, almost back to the museum, when I met

Detective John Harper walking the other way. He stopped in front of me on the sidewalk.

I was struck again by the family resemblance between him and Billy.

"Libby, how nice to see you." Short and heavy-set, he looked happier than normal. "And how is Bella doing?"

"Doing well. As usual, she's keeping the squirrel population on Elm Street nervous."

He chuckled. "I guess you've heard about the latest murders outside of town, haven't you?"

"I have. In fact, I was there when both bodies were found." I kept my voice light and neutral, hoping to hide my interest in the case.

His jaw tightened. "Since it has nothing to do with the museum, you've been keeping out of the investigation, right?"

"Uh ..."

His face fell. "Libby, you've gotten involved in several murder investigations here in town. Now you're branching out to the county?" His bushy eyebrows, which were several shades darker than his salt-and-pepper buzz cut, pinched together. "I respect that you want justice, but you have to stop. It's too dangerous."

"But I have a good suspect. Well, two good suspects. I just need to figure out which one did it."

He glared at me. "Someone has brutally murdered two people. You"—he pointed a finger at me—"need to stay out of it. If you have information that can help identify the killer, you need to tell the sheriff, my nephew Billy. He and his team of trained law enforcement officers can deal with it. Not you."

My mouth pursed up. Fine. Maybe he was right. "Okay. I'll talk to the sheriff."

"I just spotted him going into the bank a minute ago," Detective Harper said. "If you go back a couple blocks, you can catch him."

I pulled out my phone and checked the time. I did have a few minutes before I needed to go back to work. I could reheat my soup in the microwave in the museum conference room. And it might be for the best to let the sheriff deal with Chad and Jessica. Maybe there was some trace evidence on the body of one of the victims that would let him figure out which of them was the killer.

I thanked Detective Harper and turned back toward the bank.

The sheriff's financial business must have been fast. I was still half a block away when I saw him come out and walk away from me.

"Sheriff Harper!" I moved faster. "Wait."

He stopped and looked back.

I waved to catch his attention and hurried closer. "I need to talk with you about the murders out at the orchard. I've learned information you need to know."

His eyes hardened. "I told you to stay out of this!" He blew out a breath like an angry bull. "Anyway, there's no need for you to be involved." He patted his cell phone, worn on a holster on his belt, right beside his gun. "I just got a call about the case myself. I've got it all wrapped up."

"You do? You know about Francie's life insurance and the fact that she wanted to divorce Chad and told him his glory days were behind him?" My words rushed out. "Or is it Jessica, because Francie was having an affair with her husband?"

He blinked. Aha! He didn't have it all wrapped up. At least one of those bits of information was new to him.

"Nice try, Libby. I figured out the connection between you and Hannah and Noah. You're practically best friends with Hannah's aunt, Alice VanMeter. Which means you've got a vested interest in protecting Noah."

"But—"

"I'm not listening. And you should leave this to me. I'm sticking with good, old-fashioned physical evidence, evidence that stacks up nicely against Noah."

It did?

"I can see you're dying to know, so I'll tell you. One of my deputies took plaster casts of the footprints found near Francie's body. They compared them to the shoes of all the alumni staying at the orchard. Those footprints were a size 13. Too big for any of the alums. The only person involved that they fit is Noah."

"Noah lives there. His footprints are all over the orchard."

"These are running footprints." He gave me a look like he thought I was stupid. "You probably aren't aware, but they look different from footprints made when a person is walking. And running is what Noah would have done after he killed Francie because she destroyed his restaurant business in St. Louis. As for Tabitha, we believe she figured out that he did it, so he had to kill her to keep her quiet."

"But Chad and Jessica—"

He jabbed me in the chest with his forefinger. "Enough! I won't have you interfering in my cases like you do with my Uncle John."

"But—"

"I'm getting ready to hold a press conference to let people know that I'm closing in on a suspect. Just dotting my t's and crossing my i's and I'll have Noah in the county jail."

Dotting his t's? Should I explain that he had that expression backward?

No. He wouldn't listen to me.

Just like he wouldn't listen about Chad and Jessica.

I squared my shoulders. I'd done what Detective Harper asked and tried to give Billy my information. But Billy was hopeless.

He was never going to find the real killer.

Which left only one option.

Me and my friends.

Chapter Fifteen

THAT EVENING, after I got home, I realized that although I had plenty of dog food, I didn't have much food for myself. I still hadn't bought groceries, so after I fed Bella and let her out, I made myself some scrambled eggs for an early dinner. Then I ran to the store and came home with a mountain of groceries. I put them away and sat on my couch with Bella resting her head on my left foot while I pondered the case. After a few minutes, I texted Cleo to see if she had time to talk.

She did, and I soon heard her *clunk-clunk-clunking* down the stairs.

"Hey." She knocked on my door.

"Come on in."

Bella lurched to her feet and circled Cleo with her tail wagging.

Cleo bent down to pet her, and I noticed how much Bella had shed on Cleo's black pants.

"Sorry about that." I pointed to a golden swath of fur. "I'll brush her later this evening after we talk. Do you want to use my lint roller?"

Cleo waved my comment aside. "No worries." She took a seat across from me. "What's going on?"

I told her about my conversation with Billy Harper. "I still think Chad is the killer, but I need a way to prove it, solid evidence that the sheriff can't dismiss."

"I think it's Jessica, but either way you're right. We need evidence." Cleo interlaced her fingers, rotated her hands so that her palms faced out, and stretched her back against the couch. "Do you think Sam or Zeke could poke around online and learn how big the insurance policy was on Francie's life?"

"I doubt it. We don't even know what company she and Chad used for life insurance. There are lots of them."

Bella looked at me, then at Cleo, then back at me. She sighed, brought over a chew toy, and lay down near us.

Cleo ran her fingertips along her jaw. "Okay, the life insurance angle won't work. What other kind of evidence could we get?"

"This is a total long shot, but maybe there's physical evidence at the orchard that the sheriff and his deputies missed that would link one of our suspects to the murders. Both times the killer hit the victim over the head with something."

"Oh, you mean like if you found a weapon that had blood on it and Chad or Jessica's fingerprints?"

"Exactly. I'm imagining that the killer grabbed something from the farm market when they killed Tabitha. I saw some broken wooden crates inside, so like a board from one of those. I doubt they would have left the weapon in the market, and if they did, the sheriff or his deputies would have found it. But the killer might have hidden it somewhere outside near the market."

"If you found it, Billy Harper would have to listen to you."

I glanced out the window. It was already dark. "I need to go over there in the daylight. It would make any clues a lot easier to find. But I feel a bit nervous about snooping around the orchard again."

"Yeah, the whole 'I had to drop something off for Hannah' was believable, but just barely."

"What I need," I said, "is for the alums to be distracted, so that they don't even notice I'm there." I rubbed Bella's ears and pondered. "You know, Hannah and Noah want this solved. Maybe they could help me."

"I like that idea." Cleo rubbed her hands together. "Maybe they could get the alums involved in a board game or a movie."

"Let's see what Hannah says." I texted her, and she immediately offered a great suggestion. The alums had gotten permission from the sheriff to go to a restaurant half an hour away. She'd suggest they go tomorrow night. I thanked her, and she promised to let me know if it worked.

I read her response out loud to Cleo.

"That sounds good, but I still don't think you should go to the orchard alone." Cleo pulled out her phone and tapped it several times. "I can't go with you tomorrow evening. I'm completely booked."

"Maybe Sam could go with me after he gets off work. Let me check." I texted him with a brief rundown of my idea and asked if he was free to come with me.

Before he could even reply, my phone dinged with a text from Hannah.

Derek, Kate, Jessica, and Chad were thrilled with the idea of going out of town to dinner. Deputy Miller was going along with them, and Kate had even offered to buy dinner for all of the alums. They'd be leaving the orchard at four-thirty.

Sam quickly agreed to go with me. A storm was forecast for the evening, so we agreed to try to get to the orchard shortly after the alums left. I didn't usually take time off work during business hours, but just this once, I would. I could make it up the next day over lunch.

"It's all set," I told Cleo. "Sam will pick Bella and me up at four twenty."

Oh, I understood that most likely if there was physical evidence, the sheriff's deputies would have already found it, or the killer might have gone back and removed it. But maybe the killer didn't realize there was blood on the weapon. Maybe the deputies hadn't found it. And maybe I would.

Not a very encouraging plan.

But it was our best shot.

〜

The next day at four, I hurried home, let Bella out, and changed into jeans and a sweater. Although it had been warm earlier in the afternoon, when I walked home, every time I went under the shade of a tree, it felt nippy.

As he'd promised, Sam arrived at four twenty to pick up Bella and me.

Bella let out a loud woof and bolted toward the door as soon as he stepped out of his car. I grabbed my purse and jacket and opened the front door. She raced across the yard, nearly knocking Sam over in her eagerness to greet him.

"Somebody loves me." He chuckled and knelt to rub her ears and scratch her tummy.

I walked over to join them, and Sam stood and pulled me into his arms. "Hey, beautiful. Ready to go sleuthing?"

"Almost. I forgot something." I kissed him, then ran back to the house and returned with a white plastic kitchen trash bag that I stuck in my back pocket. "Now I'm ready. If we find physical evidence, I don't want us to get our fingerprints on it, but I don't want to leave it there where the rain could wash away the blood. I saw that we're supposed to get a real downpour, starting about six."

Sam nodded and opened the back door of his car for Bella.

As we drove out to the orchard, clouds gathered to the southwest, and I explained more about how I hoped to find physical evidence. With luck, the rain would hold off long enough for us to find any clues before they were destroyed.

Even though he didn't say it out loud, I could tell Sam was skeptical. But he was willing to help me simply because he wanted to be sure I was safe. Talk about a good man to have in my life.

As soon as we arrived at the orchard, Hannah jogged over from the farm market and met us in the driveway.

Sam lowered his window.

"Perfect timing," Hannah said. "The alums left with Deputy Miller about ten minutes ago, and Deputy Lewis is almost certainly asleep. You should be able to look around all you like."

"That's great." Sam turned to me. "Where do you want to start first?"

"Around the farm market."

Sam parked and we got to work. We hunted through a pile of broken apple crates behind the building. We looked under the base of some peony bushes near the driveway. And we wandered through the nearby section of the orchard as birds called to each other, perhaps warning each other of the coming storm.

We found nothing.

For a while, Bella seemed excited, sniffing along the ground, and we watched eagerly to see if she led us to a clue. But we saw nothing in the grassy area that seemed to interest her. In the end, we decided that a squirrel must have recently passed by.

"Let's look where Francie was killed," I suggested.

"Lead the way," Sam said.

I stared at the trees a while to get my bearings, then walked behind the retreat center, over the small hill, and a bit to the northwest.

Sam pointed to the edge of the orchard property, where the neat rows shifted to the oak and cedar Ozark forest, which was filled with underbrush. "Noah and Hannah keep the orchard really tidy, but if the killer just used something handy when they killed Francie, they might have found a fallen branch in those woods."

"That seems reasonable."

Sam's forehead scrunched up. "Would the bark on a branch be smooth enough to show a fingerprint?"

My stomach grew heavy. "I don't know." This plan didn't stand a chance if the weapon couldn't yield a fingerprint. But ... "Maybe a thread from the killer's clothes got caught on the bark."

Sam shot me a look of pity mixed with love.

"It could have happened," I said.

He shrugged. "Where exactly was Francie killed?"

"Over this way." I gestured, and he followed me.

We began searching the ground, looking for a branch that might have been a weapon. "See anything?"

"No."

I didn't see anything either, but Bella was sniffing at the ground and—

"Wait, Bella!" I lunged toward her and grabbed her collar. She'd found an apple core, one that was eaten almost down to nothing, and been about to gobble it down.

"Look, Sam." I turned the edge of my white trash bag inside out, wrapped it over my hand like a mitten, and used it to pick up the apple core and let it slide into the bag. "It doesn't tie the trespasser to the murder, but it does prove they were here."

"Should you take it from the scene?" Sam asked.

"Bella almost ate it. If we leave it here, another animal or a bird could eat it before the sheriff's deputies get here. I'll leave it for Hannah to give to them and tell her where we found it."

We continued searching but found nothing to prove that Chad or Jessica was the killer.

I stared down at the ground and let out a heavy sigh.

"Hey," Sam said quietly. "This search was a bit of a Hail Mary, but you're not a quitter, Libby, and that's something to be proud of."

He was kind, but no matter how hard we'd tried, we hadn't found anything useful.

Sam slid his arm around my waist, and we turned back toward where we'd parked at the farm market.

Suddenly, there was a sharp crunch behind us. Sam and I spun. "Maybe it's the trespasser!" I whispered.

Sam pointed to the closest apple trees. We each did our best to hide behind the narrow trunk of one, and I bent down and whispered in Bella's ear for her to stay and be quiet.

Through the trees, we saw a blond teenage boy walking along silently, oblivious to us, with the only sound the occasional crunch when he took a bite of an apple.

Sam pointed to his phone.

I gave him a thumbs up.

He took a photo and slid his phone into his pocket. "Now?" he mouthed.

I nodded. "Hey, wait," I yelled. "We want to talk with you."

The teen raised his head with a jerk, then turned and sprinted back in the direction he'd come from.

Sam, Bella, and I raced after him, but Sam and I quickly gave up. After looking at us panting, Bella stopped as well. That kid ran as if he was in an Olympic time trial for the fifty-yard dash.

I bent over and gasped for air. "At least you got the photo."

"We can show Noah and Hannah who their trespasser is," Sam said.

"And Noah said he thought the trespasser was coming onto the orchard property every day. He seems to walk right near where Francie was killed. And right now is about the time of the murder. Maybe Chad is right. Maybe this kid killed Francie."

Sam's eyes narrowed. "But why? I doubt he even knows her."

"We can't rule him out. We have no idea what Francie might have seen. Maybe he was meeting someone and doing something illegal."

Sam ran a hand over his jaw. "I guess it's a possibility. That kid was wearing a Dogwood Springs High School cross-country sweatshirt. I bet Zeke can identify him."

"I bet you're right." I sent Zeke a text, and three minutes later, he replied with the answer.

Chapter Sixteen

ACCORDING TO ZEKE, the trespasser's name was Eli Waller, and he was a high school senior. He lived quite close to the orchard, although Zeke said you got to the Wallers' property from another direction, from McGill Road. Eli was the star of the high school track team and ran cross country in the fall to keep in shape. He worked most evenings at Frank's Groceries, a store on the south end of town.

> **Zeke Anderson**
> U want me 2 msg him 2 see if he'll talk
> 2 u?

I asked Sam what he thought, then replied.

> No. I think the conversation would go
> better with an element of surprise. He
> acted pretty guilty today. I doubt he's
> going to talk to us willingly.

Zeke sent back a thumbs-up.

"What do you say we grab some dinner?" Sam said. "Take it back to your house to eat and then stop by the grocery store to see if Eli's working tonight."

"Sounds perfect," I said.

We left the apple core with Hannah, picked up Chinese food from a restaurant near campus, and drove to my house. I fed Bella, then I arranged our egg drop soup, General Tso's chicken, and sweet and sour pork on the table while Sam took Bella outside.

As we were eating, rain began falling. By the time we'd finished dinner, it was pouring—huge drops that seemed like they were being flung at the ground. We assured Bella we would be back soon, did our best to stay dry as we ran to Sam's car, and drove to the store.

Frank's Groceries, a small, locally owned store, had probably been in business since the 1960s. According to Sam, it was a favorite among Grove University faculty because of its excellent meat department and because it was handy to pop in and grab a thing or two after work.

Outside, the structure looked like it hadn't changed since it was built except for a recent paint job. Inside, it had worn tile floors, an old-fashioned soda machine that sold bottles, and the pervasive aroma of fried chicken. Except for the high-end specialty items I spotted on a display near the door, I felt like I'd gone back in time.

I nudged Sam and tilted my head toward the teenager working at register three. "Is that him?"

Sam pulled out his phone and looked at the photo again. "It sure is. Let's see what he has to say."

As we'd seen when he dashed away, Eli Waller had blond hair. Up close, I could see that he had hazel eyes, a rather sad excuse for a beard, and a bored expression. But when Sam and I walked up from the wrong end of the checkout aisle, his face froze, then he quickly asked if he could help us find anything.

A halfway decent attempt at playing it cool, but it wasn't going to work. I stepped closer to the register. "We're not shopping. We wanted to talk with you. We didn't have a chance earlier today out in the orchard."

Eli glanced around.

Lucky for us, the store seemed empty. If I had to guess, I'd say most of their business was the after-work traffic from the university that Sam had mentioned.

"Noah Porter told us someone has been trespassing in the orchard almost every day, stealing apples." I gave Eli a pointed stare. "We believe that trespasser is you. We even got a photo of you today."

Eli's mouth tensed.

"Francie Weaver, a news anchor from Channel 7 in St. Louis was murdered at a spot along the route you take through the orchard, right about the time that you seem to walk there." I gave him my best no-nonsense stare. "That makes you look awfully suspicious, don't you think?"

His Adam's apple rose and fell.

I leaned over the checkout lane and glanced down at his feet. "And the sheriff has a plaster cast of shoe prints found at the murder site. I'd hazard a guess that they'd fit your size 13s exactly."

Eli's mouth fell open. "You think I killed her?"

"What happened, Eli? Did she startle you? Maybe see you doing something illegal?" A possible motive popped into my head. "Meeting someone for a drug deal, perhaps?"

"Are you nuts?" Sweat broke out on his upper lip. "I didn't kill anyone. And I don't do drugs."

Then why had he run when we saw him in the orchard earlier? And why did he seem so scared now? Noah and Hannah weren't happy that he'd been stealing apples, but that wasn't enough to warrant this reaction. Unless he saw something the day of the murder... "You know the sheriff thinks Noah is the murderer, don't you?"

"Noah?" Eli's voice squeaked. "I heard the sheriff had found the killer, but I didn't hear that it was Noah." He shook his head. "Billy Harper's crazy. Noah wouldn't kill anybody, and he wasn't the person I ..."

Adrenalin shot through me. "The person you saw?"

He gave a barely perceptible nod.

I stared at him in disbelief. "If you saw the murderer, why haven't you gone to the police?"

"Because if anybody finds out why I've been going through the orchard, I'll be in big trouble."

"Bigger than Noah, who could be tried for murder?" Sam said. "He hasn't actually been arrested, but the sheriff is building his case."

Eli's eyes widened. "No, not as bad as that, but I'll lose my track scholarship to the university. My parents will be devastated. I'm supposed to be the first in my family to go to college."

"It's just a few apples," I said. "Noah and Hannah will certainly understand, especially if you help prove Noah's innocence."

"That's not it." Eli's voice was so low I could barely hear him.

"Please, we need to know what you saw," I said. "The sheriff believes Noah is the killer. If he's convicted, Noah could get the death penalty."

Eli's eyes widened. "The death penalty? Geez. If I tell you, can you keep my name out of it?"

"I can try," I said.

The boy stared down for a moment and gripped the counter so tightly that his knuckles turned white. "Okay." He let out a heavy breath. "I'll tell you."

Sam and I stepped closer.

"The day of the murder, I heard two people arguing in the orchard."

My pulse sped. "You did?"

"Yeah. That blond woman who died. I saw her picture online. And someone in a camouflage jacket with the hood up."

"Can you describe the person in the jacket?" I asked. "Man? Woman? How tall they were? Or what kind of shoes they were wearing?"

Eli shook his head. "I don't notice people's shoes. And they were facing away from me. I was trying to stay hidden behind the trees."

"Did you hear their voices well enough to identify them?" Sam asked.

"I mostly heard the blond woman. Especially when she got all sarcastic and said 'Or what? You're going to kill me?'"

I drew in a sharp gasp.

"I know." Eli winced. "But then the other person turned and went back toward the barn, and she didn't seem afraid. She was laughing. So, I left. But when I heard about it later, I figured the person in the camo jacket came back and killed her."

"You need to take this to the police," Sam said. "It's vital evidence."

"Even if you stole a hundred apples, you've got to think of Noah," I added.

"I feel bad about stealing the apples, but it wasn't just that," Eli said.

Sam and I looked at each other, then back at Eli.

"Think about poor Hannah if Noah is convicted of murder."

Eli's shoulders crumpled. "Okay, okay. I'll tell you. About two weeks ago, I was walking in the woods, all bummed because my girlfriend had dumped me for this rich kid who moved to town. There's sort of a path, probably made by deer, that starts behind our barn. Without realizing it I wandered over near Miss Pruitt's house."

"Who's Miss Pruitt?" I stepped closer.

"She's the new English teacher at the high school this year. My house is on one side of the orchard. She lives on the other." He shot a glance at Sam. "She's twenty-two, long dark hair, really hot."

Sam gave a slow nod.

"She ..." Eli squeezed his eyes shut and looked away. "She was in her hot tub, naked."

"Ahh." This was starting to make sense.

"She'd kill me if she thought I was spying on her. I got out of there as fast as I could without making any noise. But later I was playing video games online with my cousin who lives in Minnesota, and he dared me to go back the next day and get a photo." Eli shifted his weight from one foot to the other. "And the next day I went back." He lowered his gaze. "But Miss Pruitt wasn't there, and on the way home I realized how stupid I was and what a creepy thing I was doing. I told my cousin that I didn't care about the dare. I wasn't doing it."

"But you said this happened two weeks ago," Sam said. "Francie was killed last week."

"Yeah, I know." Eli shifted his weight. "The next morning, I realized my varsity track pin was missing from my letter jacket. What if Miss Pruitt found it on her land? She'd figure out what I did. I'm the only person who runs track who lives anywhere near here. So, I've been looking in the orchard each day, hoping to find it."

"Did you?" I asked.

"Not at first," he said. "But today there was a long teachers' meeting after school. They were complaining about it, so I knew she'd get home really late. As soon as I got home from cross-country practice, I ran over to look at her house, and I found it, right by where I was when I saw her in the hot tub. It's kind of broken but ..." He pulled a gold pin that looked like a little winged foot from the pocket of his jeans. The pin on the back was bent.

I glanced over at Sam.

"If Miss Pruitt thinks I spied on her, she'll fail me for sure." Eli's jaw stiffened. "So, I'm not talking to the police. No way. You can tell them what I saw, but you promised you'd keep my name out of this."

"I'll do everything I can," I said, "but part of this will be up to the sheriff."

"Oh geez." Eli grabbed his stomach. "I think I feel sick. Please, I have to keep my grades up this year, or they'll pull my scholarship. If I get an F in English ..."

"I'll do my best," I said.

Sam and I hurried back to his car, trying to avoid the puddles in the parking lot. Once we were inside with our wet umbrellas on the floor of the back seat, he looked over at me. "Well, that wasn't what I expected. I didn't have much hope for our search today, but you've found a real clue, Libby."

Delight bubbled up inside me. Maybe, just maybe, we were finally close to the truth.

Chapter Seventeen

"I'M sure the alums are back from dinner," I said as Sam pulled out of the parking lot for Frank's Groceries. "But first thing tomorrow, I need to search for that camouflage jacket. If I can find it in Chad's room—or Jessica's room—I'll have enough evidence to convince the sheriff to listen to me."

Sam glanced over at me, his eyes tensing. "That sounds good, but I've got a meeting with the dean first thing in the morning."

"You don't have to go with me."

He shot me a nervous look. "I sure don't want you going there alone."

"Zeke will be in school. Let me see if Alice or Doug or Cleo is available." I quickly typed in a text.

"How are you going to snoop around and look in people's closets with all the alums hanging out at the retreat center?" Sam said.

My excitement fizzled like a deflating balloon. "Good point." But I just knew this clue could identify the killer and provide solid physical evidence, evidence the sheriff couldn't dismiss. "Let me text Hannah. Maybe she can get the alums to leave the orchard again." I tapped at my phone.

It dinged with a text and then almost immediately dinged with a second.

"Ooh! This is perfect! Hannah, Noah, and all the alums are spending all morning tomorrow, starting at nine o'clock sharp, putting out fall decorations near the farm market. They've got hay bales, three colors of mums, pumpkins, and corn stalks, as well as decorations that Hannah ordered online. She even told me where there's a master key for all the bedrooms taped to the bottom of a drawer in the kitchen, in case one of the alums locked their door."

"All of them will be out of the retreat center?"

"That's what Hannah said. Apparently, it was Kate's idea. She feels terrible about the bad publicity the orchard is getting during its most important season. She said if the sheriff requires them to stay in Dogwood Springs, they can at least do something to help the orchard."

"Was one of those texts someone saying they can go with you?"

"Cleo. She had a cut and perm scheduled first thing tomorrow morning, but the woman canceled. She has the stomach flu."

Sam pulled up in front of my house.

"Come on in," I said. "Let's tell Cleo all the details."

We put our dripping umbrellas beside the door in the

entryway, and I called up the stairs to Cleo, then unlocked the door to my apartment.

Bella came bounding out.

"Hey, girl, look who's here to visit." I gave her a quick pat.

She let out a loud woof and immediately transferred her attention to Sam.

The entryway wasn't that large, so I went into my apartment. After a few minutes, Bella calmed down and followed Sam and Cleo in.

I explained to Cleo how the alums would be occupied and away from the retreat center, making it easy for us to hunt for the camouflage jacket. "We can search Chad's room and Jessica's and—" I blew out a frustrated breath.

"What?" Cleo said.

"I just realized. All the alums will be near the farm market. They'll see us as we drive by on the way to the retreat center."

"That's bound to make the killer suspicious," Sam said.

He was right. I hesitated, trying to figure out a way to make my plan work. "Hey! What if we went through the woods from Eli's house?"

"What's Eli's last name?" Cleo asked.

"Waller," Sam said.

Cleo's eyebrows rose. "Lives out on McGill Road?"

"Yes," I said quickly. "That's the guy."

"I know the house," Cleo said. "I didn't put it together earlier, but my dad bought a used kayak from them when I was in high school, and I went with him to pick it up. Let me look on my phone."

She used an app to find the Waller house and the orchard on a map. "We could easily sneak into the retreat center from the back." She pointed to the screen. "The alums would never know we were there."

Excellent! I loved having friends who knew the area so well. "Eli said his parents both work. He'll be at school, so no one should notice if we park at their house. He said he uses a path that starts behind their barn. I bet we can find it."

"Then we can slip in the back door of the retreat center and hunt for the jacket," Cleo said.

"And you'll both be careful, right?" Sam looked at Cleo and me.

"We will." I squeezed his hand. "What time is your meeting with the dean over?"

"Ten thirty," Sam replied.

"I'll text you as soon as we're back in the car," I said. "So you can know we're safe."

"You promise? This whole thing makes me uneasy."

"I promise." I hugged him. I was lucky to be in a relationship with a man who cared so much about me. "The minute you turn on your phone at ten thirty, you'll see my message."

"Thanks." He gave Bella another scratch between the ears, then said he had to go write an exam for tomorrow afternoon.

Cleo headed upstairs, saying she needed a good night's

sleep if she was going to help me hunt for clues in the morning.

I walked Sam to the door, kissed him goodnight, and took Bella out to the backyard one last time.

Then I sat on the back step and gazed up at the stars until Bella trotted over to me. I scratched her ears and let her inside.

"Tomorrow, girl," I said, "we're going to figure out whether the killer is Chad or Jessica!"

She wagged her tail and looked up at me, eyes gleaming.

The next morning, I put on my oldest tennis shoes and packed an old hand towel in my big purse so I could wipe off Bella's feet once we made our way to the retreat center. The rain had stopped, but the ground was soaked.

At about ten 'til nine, we headed out on our mission. Cleo drove, I watched for the address, and Bella supervised from the back.

After several curves on McGill Road, I pointed out the window of Cleo's Jeep. "Look, that mailbox says 'Waller.'"

"I'm glad you spotted it." Cleo turned into the drive of a cute ranch-style home. "I thought the house was blue."

"That tan siding looks pretty new," I said.

"I guess it has been more than ten years since I was here." Cleo parked beside the barn, and I let Bella out. Then Cleo opened the back of her Jeep and pulled out a box of nitrile gloves. "I use these for color jobs." She stuck two pairs in her back pocket. "I thought we could wear them, so we don't leave any fingerprints and get in trouble with the sheriff."

"Brilliant!"

Bella's ears perked up and she let out two loud barks.

Inside the Waller house, a big orange cat peered out at us.

Bella barked again.

The cat disappeared, and there was no other movement from the house. As we'd expected, Eli and his parents were gone for the day.

"Let's look around the back of the barn," I said.

We walked through the yard and slipped behind the barn.

Bella quickly found a place where the underbrush was flattened, and Cleo and I followed along.

We skirted a low bush and walked along a narrow, leaf-strewn path through the woods. As long as I didn't bump into the brush around me, I stayed dry. At least until the wind shook the leaves of an oak tree and sent droplets of water showering down on me, including a particularly icy one that ran down the back of my neck.

I shuddered, and a bluejay squawked in the tree above me as if he found my chill hilarious.

A couple of minutes later, after avoiding mud as best we could and climbing over a barbed-wire fence, we were in the orchard. The metal rooftop of the old farmhouse gleamed in the morning light.

I laid a finger over my lips and Cleo nodded. I whispered to Bella to be quiet.

We crept through the grassy area behind the retreat center, up onto the wooden back porch, and to the kitchen door.

"What if it's locked?" I asked.

"Why would they lock it? They're just over that ridge at the farm market." Cleo grinned. "I could see locking a bedroom if you had a computer or jewelry in there, but nobody's going to be able to steal anything big without driving by the farm market where everyone would see them."

"I guess you're right." I turned the knob, which easily gave in my hand.

We wiped and re-wiped our shoes on the mat. Two seconds later, we were inside the empty kitchen.

For a moment, we stood, barely breathing, listening for any sound from the floor above us.

But we didn't hear a thing. No conversation, no creaking boards, no running water or hair dryers. And instead of the aroma of something yummy baking in the oven, I smelled burned toast.

"I think we're safe." I set my purse on the counter and dug out the towel to clean Bella's feet. Then I found the drawer Hannah had indicated and untaped the master key from underneath. I started toward the hall, then turned back.

"Whoops, I forgot something." I grabbed my purse, dug through it, and stashed my pepper spray in my back pocket.

Cleo gave me a thumbs-up. "Let's make sure all the rooms are empty before we start searching."

"Good idea." Carefully, we checked the first floor, which was empty. Upstairs, we knocked on each door, then tried the knob. The rooms were very similar, each done in a different shade of a restful palette. One was tan, one a soft blue, one a pale green, and one mostly white. Only Kate and Derek had locked their doors. Finally, we checked the last bedroom, one that was meticulously tidy.

Cleo let out a sigh. "Nobody's here! Let's start searching!"

"I know which room is Chad's." I gestured to the room decorated in soft shades of blue. "I saw a letter jacket lying on a chair in here."

Cleo pulled out the nitrile gloves and handed me a pair.

"Thanks." I tugged them on, and the two of us began searching the room.

Chad didn't leave a lot of clutter around and instead put everything into the closet or back in his suitcase. But things weren't organized, only shoved out of sight. The clothes in the suitcase looked as if they had been stirred, and his shoes were tossed randomly in the bottom of the closet. I took a metal hanger from the closet and, as I peered in, used it to move items of clothing aside one by one.

Cleo dug through the suitcase and then checked each drawer of the dresser. "These drawers are all empty. Are you finding anything?"

"Not yet." But I wasn't giving up. I turned to Bella.

"We're looking for clues, girl. Especially a camouflage jacket."

She angled her head to one side and just stood there, looking at me.

Fifteen minutes later we'd searched everywhere in Chad's room—and in Jessica's meticulously tidy room.

Twice.

Bella lay on the floor of Jessica's room, looking bored.

"Should we look in the other rooms?" Cleo said.

"I really thought Chad or Jessica was the killer, but I guess so."

We tried Kate's room. Unlike Chad and Jessica, she'd unpacked everything into the dresser and closet. She'd also brought about twice as many clothes.

We snooped as fast as we could while still being methodical. We learned that Kate wore a size 7 1/2 shoe, traveled with a counter full of cosmetics, and shopped in some very expensive stores—but that shopping had not included a camouflage jacket.

"There's nothing here." Cleo slid a drawer shut.

"Let's look in Derek's room."

Cleo again took the dresser, and I flipped through the clothes in Derek's closet. It was about what I'd expect— khaki pants, polo shirts, a few dress shirts. Each shirt was exactly the same brand, same size, and either a long-sleeved dress shirt or a polo. Different colors, but no other variation. The man clearly knew what he liked.

Bella sniffed and pawed at Derek's suitcase, which he'd shoved in the back of the closet.

"I hope she doesn't smell a mouse back there," Cleo said.

"Me too." Or worse, my least favorite creature on earth—a spider.

I pulled the suitcase out, and my mouth went dry.

"Look." I pointed.

There, wadded up in a ball and shoved in the very back of the closet on the floor, was a camouflage jacket.

Chapter Eighteen

"DEREK." I grabbed Bella's collar to keep her from going any closer. I'd barely considered him as a suspect, but he had to be the killer. "I didn't even think about it, but when he gave Jessica an alibi by saying they were together, he also gave himself one."

"He must have secrets we don't know about," Cleo said. "Do you think that jacket is enough for him to be arrested?"

"It will be if there's some type of trace evidence on it that ties him to one or both of the murders." I patted Bella. "Good job, girl!"

I glanced down at my gloves and then, unable to resist, leaned in and picked up the jacket.

Something crackled in the pocket.

I let go of Bella's collar, reached into the pocket, and pulled out a tightly wadded piece of paper. A faint, floral fragrance escaped as I unfolded it. "It smells like lily of the valley! Like Francie!" No wonder Bella had sniffed it out.

"What is it?" Cleo stepped closer.

The two of us leaned in and read.

"Wow." Cleo let out a low whistle. "That's why he killed her, isn't it?"

"It has to be." I laid the note on the bed and snapped a quick photo.

Cleo's jaw tightened. "We'd better get out of here."

I crumpled the note back into a tight ball, returned it to the pocket, and put the jacket exactly where it had been on the closet floor. I put the suitcase back in the closet and scanned the room, making sure we had left no evidence of our snooping.

Cleo carefully re-aligned some papers on the top of the dresser. "Come on," she said, starting down the stairs.

"Let's go, Bella," I said.

My phone dinged with a text, and I pulled it from my pocket.

Sam Collins
My meeting is over. Are you okay?

It was ten thirty-two. "I have to answer this, Cleo." If I didn't, Sam would think something was wrong. I typed in a quick text telling him what we'd found as I walked to the top of the stairs.

I heard Cleo's footsteps go into the kitchen, and just as I was about to send my text, the front door opened.

I looked up, startled.

Derek walked in.

My heart sped and I missed the top step and slid down two steps before I managed to grab the railing.

But my phone hit the stairs, bounced, and plummeted through the stair rail.

"I'll get it!" Derek dove for the phone and caught it before it crashed into the tile floor. Pride and a hint of surprise flashed over his face as if he thought his athletic prowess was quite remarkable. "It seems it's rather fortunate I had to step back here for a work-related call."

"Thanks." I rushed down the stairs. "I've got a good phone case, but I doubt it's strong enough to survive an eight-foot drop onto tile." I held out my hand.

Please, I begged silently, please, please, please let him hand the phone to me face down so that he won't see the message I was about to send to Sam.

No such luck. Derek glanced at the phone, and his mouth formed a hard line. His eyes, which had shone with delight, went cold. He stepped to the base of the stairs, blocking my exit. And he calmly tapped the screen, erasing the message that explained that he was the killer.

My throat tightened.

"Miss Ballard," he said evenly, "I must commend your persistence. But rest assured, you will neither be seeking help nor leaving this place. The killer will claim another victim, and that incompetent sheriff will remain none the wiser. My academic career will not be undone by mistakes I made in my youth."

I backed two steps up the stairs.

"If you'd had any hint of good sense," he said, "you'd have stayed out of this."

Bella stood her ground. Her muscles stiffened as if she sensed, even without me saying anything, that Derek was a threat.

Which he definitely was. He moved up the first two steps, one hand on the wall, one hand on the rail. There was no way I was getting past him …

Wait! My pepper spray!

Adrenalin shot through me, and I whipped the spray out of my pocket and pressed the plunger.

He jerked back, and a rush of triumph filled my chest.

But only a weak trickle came out of the canister.

My throat grew so tight I could barely breathe. I pressed the plunger again.

Another trickle dripped onto the steps.

Derek's eyes crinkled. "Gee, Libby," he said in a syrupy voice. "Didn't you know those canisters can get clogged if you let them sit a long time? Manufacturers recommend you replace pepper spray every twelve to eighteen months." He gave me a sickening smile. "But I guess you didn't know that."

Sweat beaded all over me. I did know that, and I'd purchased the pepper spray less than six months ago.

I glanced down at the canister. Apparently, I'd bought one that should have been taken off the shelves. The expiration date was long past. And now my heart felt like it was about to pound out my chest.

I forced myself not to look back over the stairs toward

the kitchen. Maybe Cleo could save me. As long as I didn't give her position away.

And as long as her self-defense skills were in good form. But as far as I knew, she hadn't taken any classes since she'd left New York …

… five years ago.

The only thing I could do was to keep Derek's attention on me. "I read Francie's note. I can't believe you killed her just because she knew that you'd plagiarized your honors thesis as an undergrad."

"She could have ruined me!" He lurched up another step. "Back then no one could tell, but today there are plagiarism checkers that will easily find the paper I passed off as mine. They'll see the dates. They'll know mine was written later." His voice grew harder. "If only she wasn't such an interfering idiot. Like you."

Bella growled.

"You keep that stupid dog away from me," he yelled.

I glared at him. "Bella is not stupid. She's the one who found the jacket with the note."

He sniffed and looked down at Bella with disgust. "Then I might need to get rid of her as well."

Heat poured through me. There was no way he was touching Bella! I glared at him, desperately hoping that—

I spotted Cleo! She'd gone through the kitchen into the dining room, and then through the doorway from the dining room into the hall. Her eyes shone with determination as she snuck up behind Derek.

And then she raised the apple-shaped chopping board and bashed him solidly over the head.

His body crumpled, and he collapsed onto the stairs with a thud.

I let out a ragged breath. "Oh, Cleo, thank you!" She truly was the best friend ever.

Cleo crouched beside Derek. "Is he alive?"

I rolled him over and peered down at his chest, which rose and fell. "He is! Quick," I yelled. "Before he comes to, let's tie him up."

Cleo held up the chopping board. "I'll keep an eye on him. Check that big pantry in the kitchen for something we can use, maybe an extension cord."

I raced to the kitchen and, after scanning the shelves, found a roll of baling twine with some country-style wrapping paper. I grabbed a knife from the kitchen knife block to use to cut it and hurried back to Cleo.

Cleo took one leg, and I took the other, and we pulled Derek away from the stairs. His head fell from the first step to the tile floor with a *thunk*.

Cleo and I exchanged glances, and we both shrugged. It was hard to feel sympathy for a man who'd killed two people and had been ready to make me the third.

We dragged him to the living room. Then we tied his ankles and, while Bella glared at him and Cleo pulled his hands behind his back, I securely tied his wrists.

"Check for a weapon," Cleo said.

I searched the pockets of his pants and jacket. "Nope.

Phone, wallet, keys, and thirteen cents in change. And my phone." I pocketed it.

"You should take his keys and phone too."

I grabbed them and put them in my other pocket.

"I'm so glad you were here with me, Cleo." I gave her a weak grin. "You really saved me."

She shrugged.

A half-second later, the front door burst open, Bella barked, and Sam ran in. "Libby, are you okay? Ten thirty came and went and you never sent a text. I tried texting, but you didn't reply."

"I'm fine." I gestured to the floor. "Derek came back and surprised us." I pulled out my phone. Sure enough, it was set to silent. Derek must have accidentally silenced it when he caught it.

"I'm so sorry to have scared you," I told Sam, as he pulled me into a hug.

When he released me, I let out a shaky breath.

Sam led me to the couch and sat beside me. Bella lay down at our feet. And Cleo stood across from us while she and I explained what had happened.

"I guess we'd better call the sheriff." I dialed.

Thanks to the fact that Derek had caught my phone before it hit the tile floor, it still worked, an irony that I truly enjoyed. I told the 911 operator that we needed the sheriff at the old farmhouse at Witley's orchard.

I answered the operator's questions, told her we were not in immediate danger, and thanked her for staying on the line with me.

Then I noticed what time it was. Ten forty-two. Sam had texted me ten minutes ago. "How did you get here so fast?"

He gave me a sheepish grin. "I may have broken the speed limit on the way here. I thought you were in danger."

"Awww, Libby," Cleo said, "he didn't want anything to happen to you. He's got things all planned to—"

"To have you over for a nice dinner on Saturday if you're available," Sam said quickly.

I nodded.

"And now we can use it as a time to celebrate the fact that you've caught another murderer." He wrapped an arm around my shoulders and pulled me close. "I'm really glad you're all right."

"I'm sorry I frightened you."

"Just so you're safe now," he said.

My heart swelled and I savored the warmth of his embrace. This man, this wonderful man I loved, had raced over from campus because he was worried about me.

After the way my ex-husband had treated me, it had taken a long while for me to feel secure in my relationship with Sam. But once again, he had proved how much he loved me, proved that I could count on him no matter what. "Thank you," I squeezed his hand. "I can't tell you how much this means to me."

A siren wailed, growing louder with each second.

I angled my head toward Derek. "We're going to have some explaining to do to the sheriff."

"Billy Harper is not going to be happy," Cleo said. "We

didn't stay away from the orchard, and we figured out who the killer was before he did."

"Thanks to Bella." I scratched at the base of my sweet dog's ears. "She found the clue we needed."

Sam and Cleo bent down and patted Bella's head, and Sam told her she was the smartest dog in town.

She looked up at the three of us with love.

Suddenly, Derek stirred. "What have you done to me?" He moaned and squirmed to face us. "I need to go to the ER. My head hurts so much, I think I have a concussion."

"You know what?" I grinned at Sam and Cleo. "I'll be more than happy to see Billy Harper. He can be the hero who unties Derek."

"Sounds good to me." Cleo picked up the chopping board that she'd left at the bottom of the stairs. "I'll even let him use my best weapon."

Derek's jaw tightened and his face grew red.

Sam, Cleo, and I exchanged grins, and we waited for the sheriff.

Chapter Nineteen

THE NEXT DAY, right after six in the evening, my friends and I got together with Noah and Hannah at the orchard to discuss Derek's arrest.

The sun hung low in the sky, casting a golden glow over the apple trees. The weather had turned, and the air was warm, with the night's low predicted to only get down to 50.

I let out a long sigh, snuggled into my wool jacket, and sat beside Cleo, across from Sam at one of the long tables outside the barn at the orchard. The breast pocket of my jacket bulged with four new canisters of pepper spray, gifts from my friends, each canister with more than a year until it expired. I patted the pocket, grateful to feel so loved.

I'd already fed Bella at home, but after she greeted everyone, I gave her a treat. She carried it to the end of the table and flopped down on the gravel beside Alice.

Hannah unfurled a red-and-white checked cloth over the table, and Noah passed out cups of hot apple cider.

"The restaurant wouldn't even let me pay." Doug set down a large cardboard box with the Pit & Pickle Barbecue Joint logo. "Once the owner knew the meal was for our super sleuth, Libby, and her team, she wanted to say thank you for making the town safe again."

"That is so sweet of her." I took the foil-wrapped package he handed me, peeled off the top to reveal slices of brisket, and set it in the middle of the table. The aroma rolled out like a wave, and my mouth instantly began watering.

Cleo, Sam, Zeke, Hannah, Alice, and Noah each opened their own foil-wrapped packages. Within seconds, in addition to the brisket, the table was loaded with ribs, a large tub of sauce, potato skins, coleslaw, and buttery garlic bread, as well as a container of napkins and compostable utensils.

After all the unpacking, the ribs ended up near Bella's end of the table.

She stood, sniffed near the edge of the container, and only lay back down after Doug switched the positions of the ribs and the slaw, putting the ribs well out of reach.

I dug into my purse, called her over, and slipped her one more doggy treat.

"This looks fantastic, Doug," Noah said. "Thanks so much for picking it up."

Doug gestured to Alice. "It was all my brilliant wife's idea. When she learned how your business picked up as soon as word got out that the killer was in custody, she thought this would be the easiest way for us to meet after you closed the farm market for the day."

Hannah shot Alice a look of gratitude. "And you made a cobbler." She glanced around the table. "Isn't that just so like Alice?"

We murmured our agreement and our thanks.

"A cobbler seemed like the ideal use for those apples you gave me last time I was out," Alice said. "I'm really glad your regular customers are back."

"Our regular customers and then some," Noah said. "Hannah and I barely had time to catch our breath all afternoon. My guess is that over the weekend we'll be even busier."

"Did the alums all leave?" Cleo asked.

"About half an hour after the sheriff said they could. Basically, as fast as they could pack up," Hannah said. "I think they were eager to get home."

Alice opened a package of paper plates and handed some out. "Let's start passing the food. Then I want to know all the details behind the two murders."

We began filling our plates.

Zeke paused in the middle of piling ribs on his plate and looked at me. "The sheriff gave you details? Sweet."

I shook my head. "No, but between what Noah and Hannah learned and what Cleo heard at her salon, I think we have a fairly good idea of what went on."

"So, tell us the whole story," Doug said. "Why did Derek kill Francie and Tabitha?"

I poured sweet barbecue sauce over a generous serving

of brisket. "Back in college, Derek plagiarized his honors thesis. He thought the fact that he got away with it made him smarter than all of his professors."

"Oh, wow," Cleo said.

"And then," I added, "because he had a crush on Francie—"

"A huuuuge crush," Hannah added.

"He bragged about it to her." I took a quick sip of my cider. "She forgot all about it until the group decided to have their own reunion. She looked up her classmates on social media. When she learned that Derek had become a popular speaker at conferences on the topic of academic integrity, she thought it was hilarious. She started texting him, and she left that note in his room at the retreat center, saying she could destroy his career by giving the information to a journalist near where he works in Kansas."

"I'd say she definitely could have," Sam said.

I chewed a bite of garlic bread and wiped my fingers. "We'll never know if Francie was serious or just teasing, but Derek believed her. As soon as he learned about the retreat, he made plans to attend and kill her. It wasn't even his fall break. He lied about the whole thing."

"What about Tabitha?" Alice asked.

"Tabitha saw something," I said. "Maybe not the murder itself, but enough to make her suspicious. At first, Derek was able to keep her silent with threats, but after a day or so, she called the sheriff, saying she had information to give them about the murder. Derek must have overheard her and made sure she couldn't follow through."

"Man." Sam shook his head. "So, then he'd gone from one murder to two."

Zeke gestured with a rib bone he'd already picked clean. "Jessica must have known Derek was lying when he said they were together when Francie was killed. Why did she go along with that?"

"I bet I know," Hannah said. "There were several times Derek protected Jessica in college when she was afraid to stand up for herself. I bet she thought he was simply doing that again."

Cleo looked over at Hannah. "Didn't you say you thought Jessica wanted to date Derek back in college?"

"I did." Hannah's eyes narrowed. "I guess that could have played into why Jessica kept silent as well."

Chad had mentioned that Jessica reminded Derek of his younger sister. If he felt that connection, the fact that he'd protected her when they were in school made sense. But she must have been horrified when she learned that her protector—the person she'd once wanted to date—was the killer.

"I really thought Jessica was the culprit," Cleo said. "But I was wrong."

I shrugged. "These murders were confusing. For a while, I even suspected Kate when Derek suggested she was the killer. She did find the body, and she did arrange the extra reunion days at the orchard. And she gave Francie an odd look when she introduced me to her. But I talked with Kate today. She didn't remember for sure, but she said that most likely she had that look because—although she had managed to overlook Francie's arrogance in college—as an adult, she had no patience for it."

"What happens to Derek now?" Zeke asked.

"He's trying to fight the charges," I said. "But there was trace evidence on the camouflage jacket that's very incriminating. And the note. Plus, Cleo and I both heard him threaten to kill me and admit to killing Francie. And the sheriff thinks he and his team can get access to their texts and build an even stronger case."

Sam sat back and tilted his head to one side. "He's listening to his team?"

"He is," Cleo said. "I ran into Deputy Miller at the drugstore. Detective Harper had a long talk with Billy. He told him that he needed to use all the resources his department has to solve cases and that a good leader doesn't work alone."

"That's for sure," Sam said.

"The detective also suggested Billy sign up for continuing education on criminal investigations and team management," Cleo added, "and Billy agreed."

"That's encouraging," Noah said. "In spite of the fact that he arrested me, I sort of like Billy. Maybe with more training and some coaching from his uncle, he can become a good sheriff."

I had to respect Noah for his attitude. Hopefully, he was right.

"You know what I don't understand?" Cleo leaned in. "When you look at Derek's personal style, he doesn't seem like he'd wear a camouflage jacket."

"Good catch." Leave it to Cleo to pick up on the fashion aspect of the case. "He actually bought that jacket on purpose, a size too big, thinking he could use it to frame Noah or Chad. But he must have realized that forensics might tie it back to him."

"And then he didn't know what to do with it. I guess he planned to take it home," Alice said.

"He didn't count on us sneaking into his room," Cleo said.

"Or Bella finding that jacket," Zeke added.

Bella walked over to Zeke, head high, and he ran his hand along her back.

Cleo grinned. "And Derek sure didn't count on getting whacked in the head with that chopping board."

"Like the sheriff, he underestimated Libby," Sam said. "I imagine they both thought they were smarter than her." His eyes twinkled as he smiled at me. "It's always a mistake to underestimate a determined woman."

"Especially when she has a whole team of her friends and the smartest dog in town helping her." I looked around the table.

The friends Hannah had found in college had turned out to have not one, but two bad apples in the bunch—Francie with her selfish, cruel nature, and Derek, a man who was willing to commit murder. Luckily, when Hannah married Noah, she'd found a good person.

And luckily for me, the friends I had made in Dogwood Springs were wonderful people. Alice and Doug, both so kind and generous. Zeke, who was growing up more each day, becoming a man of integrity and intelligence. Cleo, the most wonderful best friend I could ever hope to have. Bella, so smart and sweet and loving. And Sam ... well, the longer we were together, the more I realized how special he was and how treasured he made me feel.

I took another sip of my hot apple cider, and the warmth of the drink felt as if it swirled around my heart. I was so incredibly fortunate.

We continued eating, and Hannah answered my questions about the early days of the orchard, back when horses and humans provided all the work, and told me how her ancestors struggled but managed to survive the Great Depression.

The food from the Pit & Pickle disappeared quickly, with Zeke volunteering to eat the last remaining rib. "It probably would go bad by tomorrow if you stuck it in the fridge," he said in a tone of false concern, then laughed.

"So generous of you." Cleo rolled her eyes. "Just make sure you don't get too full for cobbler."

He looked at her in mock horror. "I could never be too full for Alice's cobbler," he said, all humor gone. Apparently, Alice's baking was no laughing matter.

"How about a hayride?" Noah waved a hand to the tractor and wagon parked next to the barn. "And the firepit is ready if you all would like to eat your dessert around a bonfire."

"I always keep vanilla ice cream in the freezer," Hannah said. "I can go grab it."

"That sounds wonderful," I said, and my friends quickly agreed.

Five minutes later I was in the wagon, sitting on a hay bale, snuggled up next to Sam with Bella at my feet. Noah volunteered to go get the ice cream, walk down, and start the fire. Alice carried the cobbler on her lap. Cleo took charge of the paper bowls, spoons, and napkins that Hannah brought out. And Hannah climbed up on the tractor.

"Everybody ready?" she called out over the sound of the engine.

"Ready!" we said in unison.

The tractor lurched forward, and we slowly rolled through the orchard, slowing atop hills where the views were the most breathtaking. The last rays of the sunset began to fade, the sky shifted to a deep blue, and a sense of peace welled up inside me.

The killer was behind bars. The orchard was safe. And the people of the Dogwood Springs area could go back to their normal, happy lives.

In this little town, I'd encountered the worst of humanity, people willing to commit murder. Maybe it was the contrast with those rare bad apples that made me appreciate the rest of the people in the town even more.

Because Dogwood Springs was, overall, a place where neighbors helped neighbors, where tourists found rest and restoration, and where kindness and concern for all was a way of life. And it was a place I was grateful to call my home.

Hannah pulled the wagon up near the bonfire, and Sam and Bella hopped off the back. Sam lifted me down, holding me in his arms for an extra second or two before he let my feet touch the ground. I gave him a quick kiss, and we joined the others.

Old-fashioned metal lawn chairs—the kind that are built to rock slightly—surrounded a large bonfire.

"The wind's from the south." Noah gestured. "You'll want to sit on this side."

We scooted our chairs to form a half circle on the side without smoke and edged in close to the warmth of the fire. Then Alice and Cleo fixed bowls with large chunks of cobbler and generous scoops of ice cream, and I passed them out.

When everyone was served, we sat around the fire, enjoying how the flavors of cinnamon, sugar, nutmeg, and rich vanilla ice cream enhanced the tart apples. Conversation ebbed and flowed and sometimes we all sat silently, appreciating the peace of the orchard and the mesmerizing spell of the dancing fire. Bella lay in the grass between Sam and me, half asleep.

After a while, Zeke pointed up at the sky. "Look."

I tipped up my head. "Oh, it's beautiful." I'd been so busy eating and enjoying the fire that I hadn't noticed that the stars had come out.

A million points of light sparkled magically above us, shining down on our bonfire, on the orchard, and on the little town of Dogwood Springs that we called home.

"It's amazing," I said.

"Like you," Sam whispered to me.

I reached for his hand and held it tightly, my heart full of gratitude. Not only did I have this wonderful night with my friends but also the special dinner Sam was making for the two of us.

Secretly, I suspected that he was going to tell me that night about the contribution he was planning to make to the museum's new capital campaign.

I smiled to myself. Even though I'd overheard his conversation with Cleo, I'd do my best to act surprised.

Epilogue

TWO DAYS LATER, it was such a lovely Saturday morning that I wanted to be outside. Tomorrow, Cleo and I would decorate the house for Halloween, but today I had the whole day free. It was still a little early, but I grabbed my phone and dialed Sam's number.

It rang five times, and just as I thought he might still be asleep, he picked up.

"Hi, Libby." He sounded short of breath. Maybe he'd rushed out of the shower to get the phone.

"Would you like to go out to Dogwood Springs Park with me and Bella today? We could take a Frisbee and walk around the spring."

"I'd love to, but I'm swamped today. Lots of, uh, stuff for work."

"Oh." He sure was having a hard semester.

"You go ahead. You can tell me all about it tonight. You and Bella are still coming over for dinner, right?"

"I'll be there at six like you said. But if that nice dinner you were planning to make is too much trouble with all the stuff you need to do for Grove University, we could meet for pizza."

"No, no, you need to come here. I want to cook. And I want to see Bella. I'll just be busy earlier."

Cooking after a hard day didn't make much sense to me, and he sounded really stressed, but I wasn't going to argue with him. "Okay. I'll see you this evening."

From Sam's end of the line, I heard a loud *clunk*. "I, uh, I better go, Libby. See you tonight."

I hung up and looked down at Bella, who sat beside me. "Weird, Bella. Very weird. It looks like it's just you and me."

Bella wagged her tail, and I began packing things we'd want at the springs. Her Frisbee, a water bottle, an apple for me, and a doggy treat for her. We were going to have a great morning.

At six o'clock on the dot, with Bella already fed, the two of us headed up the long driveway to Ashlington. The sun was sinking behind the two-and-a-half-story Victorian, giving its exterior a rosy glow. The turret, the twin chimneys, the gingerbread trim—every detail of the old house was suffused with charm in the evening light. And the hills behind the house were filled with trees with red and orange and gold leaves, as well as a scattering of dark green cedars. I was struck, as I often was, by how wise my ancestors had been to build on such a beautiful spot. And how smart Sam had been to buy the place from my aunt.

"Ready to see Sam, Bella?" I navigated the last curve before the house.

Bella gave an enthusiastic woof.

I parked near the garage, grabbed my purse, and got out. I was just opening the back door for Bella when I could have sworn that I heard Cleo laugh. I even glanced around, but mine was the only car in the driveway.

I shook my head to clear out the confusion. All that thinking I'd done trying to figure out who the murderer was must have frazzled my brain. I'd probably heard a bird. "Come on, Bella. Let's go inside."

Before I even knocked, Sam opened the door and called hello to me. However busy his day had been, he seemed delighted to see me. And he looked fantastic in what I thought was a brand-new sweater, or at least one I'd never seen him wear. It was navy blue, perfect with his dark hair and chocolate brown eyes.

Bella nuzzled her head against the leg of his jeans, and he reached down to scratch her ears. "Hello to you too, Bella." He gestured toward his entryway. "Come on in."

I stepped inside and inhaled deeply. "It smells fantastic in here. What are we having?"

"A green salad with homemade blue cheese dressing, beef stroganoff, and sourdough bread I picked up at the bakery downtown."

"Yum! And let me guess, are we having Minnesota's Pride ice cream for dessert?"

"We just might be." Sam winked at me and led me through the kitchen. "The weather's been so nice I thought we could eat out on the patio."

"Sounds good to me."

"Come on out," he said.

An odd expression flashed through his eyes. Was he afraid it would cool off before we finished eating? Based on the weather forecast I'd seen I really didn't think so. We were having a nice warm spell.

Sam gestured for Bella and me to lead the way to the stone patio, but as I went outside, my footsteps slowed.

Fairy lights lined the limbs of the dogwood trees that surrounded the patio, shining white against the trees' red leaves. Two rows of white candles in hurricane lanterns lined a path leading to a small table at the back of the patio. Red rose petals covered the path, and on the table, more candles surrounded a huge vase of red roses.

My stomach went all fluttery, and I glanced at Sam.

He took my hand. "It seems like we should follow the path, don't you think?"

I gave a shaky nod and walked with him.

Near the table with the vase of roses, Sam stopped, rested a hand on Bella's neck, then tipped her chin up to face him. "It's time for what we practiced, girl. Go get the surprise." He pointed toward a cluster of dogwoods.

Bella trotted behind one of the trees and came back with a cardboard box about the size of a hardback book, wrapped in white paper with a big white bow. She brought it to Sam, and he took the package and handed it to me.

"Would you like to open this?" he asked softly.

"Sure." A jittery feeling bounced through me, and the sweet scent of the roses enveloped me.

Bella moved in closer, clearly ready to help with the unwrapping if needed.

I slid off the paper—which only had a small amount of doggy drool on it—and lifted the lid from the box. Inside, I found a smaller box, and inside that, a dark blue velvet ring box. Sam gently took the ring box from my hand and opened it, displaying a stunning diamond ring. Then he dropped to one knee.

I placed a hand over my pounding heart.

"Libby," he said, "spending time with you has made me happier than I've ever been. You've made my life so much richer that I can't imagine a day without you. Will you marry me?"

Excitement shot through me like fizzy champagne. "Yes," I said breathlessly. "Yes, I'll marry you, Sam."

His face burst into a smile, his eyes shone, and he slid the ring onto my finger.

My chest was hollow, filled with nothing but wonder, and my brain felt buzzy, almost numb. I'd thought I known the surprise Sam had been planning, but I'd been totally wrong. It wasn't a contribution to the museum's capital campaign. It was much, much more—the promise of a lifetime of love.

Then everything happened at once. Sam kissed me, Bella started barking, and Cleo, Alice, Doug, and Zeke surrounded us, all cheering and shouting congratulations.

I looked from one of my friends to another. "Where did you come from?"

"We were hiding in the garage." Cleo angled her head back toward the house. "Sam cracked the door to the kitchen, so when we heard you come in the front door, we snuck around the side of the house."

I shook my head at Sam. "I had no idea you had all this planned!" He'd made the proposal so romantic. He'd even found a way to include our friends—my Dogwood Springs family—and my dear, sweet Bella.

"I can't believe I pulled it off," Sam said.

"When I called this morning, you did sound stressed," I said.

"I was trying to get the lights up in the trees." He pointed to the tallest dogwood. "That one was a real challenge. But it was nothing compared to losing the ring."

"You lost the ring?" I stared down at it in shock. The white gold setting looked antique, probably from about 1910, and featured small diamonds along ribbon-like brackets on either side of the center diamond, which was enormous, at least two carats.

Sam rubbed the back of his neck. "Remember when Bella came over because you were having work done at your apartment?"

I nodded.

"I had the ring out on my coffee table because I was taking a picture of it to send to my mom. She really wanted to see it. Right before you drove up, I stepped into the other room to get the paper with all the information about the history of the ring so I could send her a photo of that too. When I came back, the ring was gone."

"Oh, no." I glanced back down at it. I already loved it and couldn't imagine it being lost.

"After you left, I looked everywhere. I thought I'd heard a metallic rattle, but I wasn't sure. After that peanut butter cookie incident, I was afraid Bella had eaten it."

"That's why I started my exercise craze," Cleo said. "I took her for her morning walks because I was on pooper scooper duty. And I collected the pooper scooper bags you put in the trash and scanned the backyard in case you missed anything. I hid all the bags on my side of the garage, just in case."

I burst out laughing. I'd been totally clueless that Cleo's sudden exercise kick had been all about helping make this wonderful day happen, even if it meant serving on pooper scooper duty.

Now that was friendship! "Did she really eat the ring?"

"No," Sam said. "I think she swished it off the table with her tail because it was finally found in the heating vent. It took the HVAC team longer than they expected, but they found it."

"Which meant no one needed to go through the pooper scooper bags," Cleo said.

I laughed again and looked at the ring.

"Do you like it?" he asked.

"It's beautiful!" I held out my hand, admiring the way the diamonds sparkled in the candlelight. "I love it."

"I'm so glad—and so glad you said yes." He kissed me

again. "I hate that this past week I've been swamped with alumni stuff at work."

I brushed his worries aside, still slightly dazed by his proposal.

"Time to pose." Cleo pulled out her phone. "We've got lots of photos to take!"

"And I made you two a cake for after dinner," Alice said. "Hold on." She dashed inside and returned with a two-layer cake, smooth along the sides, with the entire top covered in white frosting roses. It might have been decades since she'd worked in a grocery store bakery, but she'd kept her skills sharp.

"It's gorgeous, Alice," I said.

She beamed at me and gave me another hug.

"It will go great with Minnesota's Pride ice cream," Sam said.

Everyone chuckled.

Then Cleo took photo after photo, posing Sam and me by the cake, by the roses, kissing, admiring my ring, with Bella, and one especially cute one with Sam holding a sign Cleo had made that read "She said yes!"

Doug nudged Alice. "Time for us to leave and let the engaged couple have time alone, don't you think?"

"Goodness, yes." Alice hugged us both, and Doug shook Sam's hand and clasped both of mine.

Cleo gathered us both into her arms, her eyes teary, and Zeke hugged us and told us congratulations.

Then it was just Sam and me, standing on the patio. The sun had dipped below the horizon, the candles glimmered, and Bella lay on the stone patio beside us, worn out from all the excitement.

I shook my head and looked at him. "Wow, it hardly seems real."

"I'm so happy," Sam said. "My beautiful Libby, who's going to be my bride." He tipped his head toward the house. "I know we've got a while to decide, but would you like to join me living here at Ashlington after we're married?"

I gave him a wide smile. Would I like to live at Ashlington, the house my ancestors had built—the house where my mother had grown up? "What could be more perfect?"

"I'm glad you think so. I do too. And I can't wait to spend the rest of my life with you,"—he reached down to scratch my sweet dog's ears—"and with Bella."

I gazed out over the hills, barely visible in the darkness. My life felt so perfect, so incredibly perfect ...

Except for one little question that popped into my mind —the diary. "Maybe one day we'll even find that diary that Hattie hid in the fireplace at the yellow house."

"Oh! With everything that's been going on, I forgot to tell you," Sam said. "I got a call from that potential heir, a guy named Quinten. He's confident he will inherit the house, and he says when he does, he'll call me and let us look for the diary. He's really intrigued."

"Did he think it would be soon?"

"It sounded like at least a month, maybe two." Sam wrapped an arm around my waist, pulled me closer, and looked into my eyes. "In the meantime, I'm going to kiss my beautiful fiancée."

My heart swelled, and I slid my arms around his neck. "That sounds like a grand idea."

And it was.

Thank you for reading this book!

Are you ready to return to Dogwood Springs for another cozy mystery? Join Libby, Bella, and their friends in the next book in the series, *Books, Betrayal & Blame.*

A stolen manuscript, a murdered donor, and a library full of suspects.

When a rare original manuscript is set to be given to the

library in Dogwood Springs, historian Libby Ballard is among those excited to celebrate the literary treasure. But before the event begins, the book vanishes without a trace—and the donor is found murdered.

As the town reels from the shocking news, whispers and theories abound. The police have their suspect, but Libby fears the woman may have been wrongly accused, leaving the real killer walking away free. Determined to see justice served, Libby begins digging into a tangle of family drama.

With her loyal golden retriever, Bella, by her side and her friends ready to help, she starts putting the pieces together. But as the mystery deepens, so does the danger. Someone in town is hiding the truth—and they'll do anything to keep it buried.

Can Libby identify the killer before another deadly chapter is added to this tale?

Visit Dogwood Springs to start solving this mystery with Libby and Bella!

If you like a cozy mystery with a pet who will win your heart, friends who feel like family, and a hint of romance, you'll love Books, Betrayal & Blame.

Want a little extra time in Dogwood Springs? Join Sally's cozy mystery newsletter to:

- download the Dogwood Springs prequel, *BED &*

BREAKFAST & BURGLARY, free when you sign up

- enjoy exclusive bonus content for every book in the series, such as a scene from Bella's point of view
- hear about new releases and cozy extras!

Visit Sally's website at www.sallybayless.com/free-mystery/ to join.

See all the books in the Dogwood Springs Cozy Mystery Series at www.sallybayless.com.

Acknowledgments

This was a really fun book to write! A visit to an orchard is such a quintessential fall experience, filled with delights for all the senses, that it was easy to feel like I was right there amid the apple trees when I was writing the first draft.

No matter how fun creating that first draft was, though, it takes a lot to change a rough draft into a finished book. I am incredibly fortunate to have wonderful people who help me with that process.

First, a big thanks to all my readers, especially those who send me email or connect with me on social media. It's such a joy to have someone tell me they enjoy a story I've written!

Thank you to my author friends, my virtual work colleagues who make writing more fun. Whether it's a Clubhouse call discussing marketing, a one-on-one Zoom meeting when I need advice as I try something new, or our morning Teams writing sprints, you provide the social aspect of the "social creative" job I was told I needed when I was in college. The cozy author world is such a wonderful workplace!

Special thanks to fellow author Brook Peterson, whose

family are apple growers and who answered my technical questions about the business.

As always, I am so very grateful for the help I received from my wonderful beta readers: Betsy Anderson, Laurel Bayless, Debbie Edwards, Barbara Hackel, Janice Huwe, Martha Long, Kim Lyons, Carrie Saunders, and Stephanie Smith. You made this book so much stronger and more enjoyable!

Thanks to Tegan Maher of Magical Words Editing for line editing this book and to Donna Lynn Rogers of DLR Cover Design for creating the gorgeous cover. I am so lucky to get to work with both of you!

And last, but certainly not least, I'm grateful to my family—Dave, Michael, and Laurel—for their support and encouragement. Thank you!

If, in spite of the efforts of all these people, mistakes snuck in, please know that they are mine alone.

About the Author

After many years away, Sally Bayless lives in her hometown in the Missouri Ozarks. She's married and has two grown children. When not working on her next book, she enjoys reading, BBC mysteries, word puzzles, swimming, and shopping for cute shoes.

www.ingramcontent.com/pod-product-compliance
Lightning Source LLC
Chambersburg PA
CBHW032158190726
48289CB00007BA/2287